REVENGE!

Slocum's anger burned like a forest fire and tore at his guts. And there wasn't a damned thing he could do about this slaughter. He watched one cowboy go over and urge his horse to kick at the fallen vaqueros. Then he lifted his pistol and began firing rapidly into the air. The cattle finally got it through their dim brains that they should run from this annoyance.

They stampeded, trampling the fallen bodies. Slocum tugged at his horse's reins. There was nothing he could do now against Hale's men. Jorge and Tomás were dead. But Slocum would return to settle the score.

OTHER BOOKS BY JAKE LOGAN

JAKE LOGAN

SLOCUM AND THE EL PASO BLOOD FEUD

BERKLEY BOOKS, NEW YORK

SLOCUM AND THE EL PASO BLOOD FEUD

A Berkley Book/published by arrangement with
the author

PRINTING HISTORY
Berkley edition/December 1987

ISBN: 0-425-10489-3

A BERKLEY BOOK ® TM 757,375
Berkley Books are published by The Berkley Publishing Group,
200 Madison Avenue, New York, N.Y. 10016.
The name "BERKLEY" and the "B" logo
are trademarks belonging to Berkley Publishing Corporation.

PRINTED IN THE UNITED STATES OF AMERICA

10 9 8 7 6 5 4 3 2 1

1

John Slocum leaned away from his horse and spat out a mouthful of West Texas dust. He had been on the trail, riding up from San Antonio, for so long that more grit than spit came out. He wiped his mouth and straightened in the saddle, his green eyes slowly scanning the gentle slope leading down from the Hueco Mountains and into the rocky bowl that held El Paso like a tiny adobe jewel.

On the far horizon he saw the Franklin Mountains rising through a veil of distance and brown haze, but he wasn't intending to go that far. His needs outweighed the need to keep riding. Somewhere in the sleepy border town he would find a decent saloon and wet his whistle. He tried spitting again and failed. Slocum shook his head tiredly. The trail had been too long for him this time. Not only had he fought off a band of drunken Comanches just west of Abilene, he had been forced to shoot a Texas Ranger—also drunk, and doubly dangerous because of it.

Van Horn had turned too hot for him when the Ranger company commander came up from Odessa to check on his man. The only good thing Slocum could say about his ride from the south was that he had avoided the Indians and no one had got a good look at him—not good enough to give a description to the Rangers. Slocum had no desire to cross them for any reason. And right now seemed even worse since they'd got their asses kicked in the Great El Paso Salt War and were touchier than a sunburned rattlesnake.

That sorry defeat made the Rangers edgy and quicker than ever to anger. The one in Van Horn had taken offense when Slocum hadn't taken his hat off when entering the deserted saloon. "Show some respect," the Ranger had said.

It had been damned close to the last words he had ever uttered. Slocum had seen no reason to take off his hat. The Ranger reaching for his Colt had been a damnfool thing to do. The lawman lay dead on the dirty saloon floor before the barkeep could come rushing in from the back room.

Slocum took off his dusty Stetson and brushed off the brim. A tiny cloud formed. He shook it hard. He tried to obey the law when it suited him, but he never gave in to fools or thieves. Life was too short to be wasted like that.

Slocum put his heels into the strong black stallion's flanks and started the horse across the flats for El Paso. He crossed the stagecoach tracks leading north to Hueco Tanks. He paid them no mind. His path took him to a place where he could find a soft bed, a drink of whiskey, and maybe a willing woman at a decent price.

Hat pulled low to shield his eyes from the setting sun, Slocum entered the easternmost edge of El Paso. Low adobe houses stretched along the narrow streets. He kept riding. This wasn't his kind of place. What he sought was closer to the center of town.

He rode down the main street. A crudely lettered sign proclaimed this to be El Paso Street. Slocum snorted and shook his head. No imagination, even here on the edge of nowhere. When he saw the crossing street was named San Antonio he laughed outright. Several men lounging along the wooden sidewalks stared at him, but no one spoke. Their neutral, dead eyes showed no curiosity or challenge. They saw him, he saw them, and that was enough.

He rode on, past a barnlike structure at the west corner of El Paso Street and First that had a freshly painted sign on it proclaiming it to be the Coliseum Saloon and Variety Theatre. A playbill showed the type of entertainment a patron might indulge in, once inside.

Slocum reined back and studied the advertisements pasted a long the stark whitewashed walls. NINE ROOMS, one proclaimed. Gambling, keno, blackjack, faro all in one room. Dramatic plays in another. French chorus girls in a third room.

Slocum snorted and wiped dust from his lips. He had no desire to see men and women gussied up and painted like Comanches on the warpath prancing around. The part about exotic French dancing girls drew his attention, but not much. He reckoned few, if any, had ever been farther east than the Arkansas River. France to anyone dancing in the Coliseum was probably only a name or a faded drawing on a wall done by someone with more imagination and worldliness.

The Coliseum might interest him later. He was sure some of those advertised nine rooms were devoted to the cribs, but it didn't matter one whit at five in the afternoon, because the Coliseum was closed.

Across the street, the Ben Dowell Saloon was open. The swinging doors still quivered from the last eager patron to enter, or maybe the gusty wind moved them to and fro. Slocum inhaled deeply and caught a whiff of the whiskey-and-stale-beer odor from inside. This was what he needed after such a long and tiring ride. He rode around back and found a stable for patrons' horses.

"Take care of him, will you?" he called out to a stable-boy. The lad jumped to his feet, his head bouncing up and down as if on a spring.

"Yessir, anything you say, sir," the boy babbled. Slocum wondered if he looked that ornery. He knew the way he carried his ebony-handled Colt Navy in the cross-draw holster made it obvious that he was accustomed to using it. The worn grips only confirmed any such suspicion when anyone got close enough to see. But there had to be more than this. He hadn't ridden into town shooting at anything that moved.

"What makes you so edgy, son?" he asked, fishing a dime from his vest pocket and flipping it to the youth.

"Nothing, sir. Not a damn thing, no sir."

Slocum shook his head. Whatever had the stablehand spooked kept his tongue tied in knots. Slocum went into the Ben Dowell Saloon's side door and stopped to look around. In the far corner four men played cards. From the way they held their hands he knew he might have to join them later. Easy pickings should never be passed up. These were cowhands who enjoyed the whiskey and the company and didn't know a damned thing about odds.

But that could wait. He bellied up to the bar and rapped his knuckles on the highly polished surface to get the barkeep's attention. The man turned from the cowhand he was speaking to, stroked his mustache tips into place with another dollop of grease, and then came ambling down the length of the bar in no particular hurry to serve Slocum.

"You look like a man with a powerful thirst," the barkeep said.

"Sun's getting hot," Slocum allowed. "Still not summer, but it's hard to tell the difference."

"Hell, man," the barkeep said, "it'll get so hot out there in summertime that the rocks will start to melt and the lizards will cook in their own skins."

"You've talked me into a whiskey," Slocum said.

"All we got is trade whiskey." The barkeep looked toward the back of the saloon, as if checking to be sure that the owner wasn't around. "A man like you wouldn't like it."

Slocum had run into this before. The barkeep got a cut of anything special he sold. "What do you recommend?"

"Tequila *y cerveza*. The only fit drink in the whole damn place," the barkeep said, the tips of his thin, waxed black mustache wiggling as he spoke.

"Do it," said Slocum. He didn't care what he drank as

long as it was wet. The bartender pulled out a bottle and poured a shot of clear liquor, then drew a mug of foamy warm beer and put it down on the bar beside the shot of tequila.

Slocum knocked back the fiery liquor and chased it with the beer. For a few seconds nothing happened. Then he gasped. It felt as if a mule had kicked him in the belly.

The barkeep laughed and poured another. "First one's on the house. You got to take responsibility for any you drink beyond that."

Slocum gestured that he wanted the entire bottle. The bartender smiled and walked back to the far end of the bar, where he continued his conversation with the cowboy.

Slocum worked on his thirst, feeling his head spin as he drank. The tequila was potent, but he was up to it. The beer quenched his thirst and made the tequila seem almost bearable. His aches and pains from being so long in the saddle began to vanish and his attention turned back to the others in the saloon. A drunken bellow and the loud crashing of the swinging doors leading out onto El Paso Street made him swing about to see what the commotion was about.

The glint of red sunlight reflecting off the newcomer's badge held his full attention. Slocum turned back to the bar, his hand moving slowly to his Colt. He slipped the leather thong that held the gun in place off the hammer. He was ready now, if the marshal had come to arrest a Texas Ranger's killer.

Slocum relaxed and grinned at his own suspicious nature when the marshal leaned heavily against the bar and yelled, "Gimme a whiskey, Jake. Get your lazy ass over here and give me a whiskey. Keepin' the peace is a powerful thirst-making job."

"Anything you say, Marshal." Jake winked broadly to Slocum as he poured the marshal a shot. The liquor flowed sluggishly. Slocum wondered what had gone into it to give it such muddy consistency. He swallowed another shot of tequila and thanked his lucky stars that the barkeep had played straight with him. To drink that swill would have taken an iron gut.

The marshal didn't seem to mind. He drank the trade whiskey as if it was good and banged the empty glass on the bar until Jake filled it again. Slocum didn't see any money changing hands. That put the situation in El Paso into perspective. The law got what it wanted for free in El Paso—or made life hell for anyone crossing the marshal.

Slocum worked at his beer. He had seen this before, too many times before. After the War, he had lost his family farm to a Reconstruction judge who took a fancy to the rolling green hills in Calhoun County, Georgia. Back taxes, the crooked judge had declared as he foreclosed on the property. Justice, Slocum had declared as he rode away, leaving behind a fresh grave on the ridge above the springhouse.

Another man entered the saloon. Slocum's eyes narrowed at the sight of a swarthy vaquero who stared boldly at everyone in the saloon. The huge silver conches, the fine fabric of his vest, the inlaid handle of his six-shooter, the intricate hand-tooled leather holster all bespoke wealth. This was no ordinary Mexican cowhand come across the border from Paso del Norte. No peon could afford a single conch or jingling silver-chased spur in a hundred years of scrabbling on arid farmland.

"Hey, you," the marshal called out. "Who the hell you think you are, you dumb greaser? You can't come into a white man's saloon. Get your butt out of here!"

"Take it easy, Marshal Campbell," Jake said, looking nervous. The expression on his face told Slocum all he needed to know. Trouble was coming. Fast.

"I will go in a moment, *Señor* Marshal," the man said in a low, intense voice. His dark eyes worked back and forth as if he expected to find whatever he sought lurking in the shadows.

Slocum was taken by surprise when the marshal bellowed, pulled out his Colt, and swung the heavy gun down in a vicious arc that ended on the tall crown of the vaquero's sombrero. The soft felt collapsed and the pistol crunched into head bone beneath. The vaquero jerked and sank to his knees, stunned.

The marshal staggered back, regained his balance, and kicked out as hard as he could. The tip of his boot caught the Mexican on the side of his jaw. His head snapped back and he fell face down through the swing doors. He lay without stirring.

"Damned greasers don't own this town. George Campbell'll show 'em who's boss around here." The marshall downed another shot of whiskey to brace his courage, then went to the fallen man and began kicking him in the ribs.

Slocum stiffened. He reached for his pistol but felt a restraining hand on his arm.

Jake said softly, "Marshal Campbell's got a mean streak in him a mile wide when he gets drunk. Don't go crossin' him or he'll lay you out just like he did that vaquero."

"How often does he get drunk?" asked Slocum, even though he knew the answer.

Jake smiled crookedly, his mustache tips beginning to droop. "Don't reckon I ever seen him sober. Leastways, not since Judge Magoffin and the other town aldermen appointed him marshal a couple months back."

George Campbell reached down and caught the vaquero under the arms and dragged him out into the dusty street. The marshal began to kick and beat the unconscious man, venting uncontrolled drunken anger on the vaquero.

Slocum looked over at Jake, then pulled free. The tequila had been good, the beer hadn't been too flat to be undrinkable, and Jake had warned him about the whiskey. Slocum dropped a cartwheel on the bar and said, "Thanks for the liquor—and the advice."

"Shame you won't be takin' more of the latter."

"You might be right," Slocum said, but he saw the grin splitting Jake's face. The barkeep didn't care for the marshal's behavior any more than Slocum did. Hand on the ebony handle of his Colt Navy, Slocum went through the swinging doors and onto the splintery wood sidewalk running the length of the saloon.

He glanced up and down El Paso Street. Some activity had started inside the Coliseum, but not much. No one paid heed to the marshal as he savagely beat the fallen Mexican. A few men were in front of the newspaper office in the other direction. Slocum sucked in a deep breath and let it out slowly. The *El Paso Herald* was about to get a headline, whether they knew it or not.

"Don't go beatin' on him like that," Slocum said, his voice low and menacing.

"What? What's that you say, boy?" Marshal Campbell swung around and almost lost his balance. He got his feet under him and stood in a wide stance, his hand on his pistol butt, as if he could threaten anyone looking as he did. "Who are you to go tellin' the duly appointed law around here what to do? You ain't one of those damn Texas Rangers Captain Baylor's sent up from the Marsh Ranch, are you?"

"I don't like to see you treating anyone like that—and for no good reason."

"You got no call tellin' me what my job is, boy."

"You start to pull that rusty gun of yours and you're buzzard meat," Slocum said.

George Campbell looked more surprised than afraid. Slocum guessed that was the liquor's fault. Nobody saw the set of Slocum's body or the flinty hardness in his cold green eyes and looked surprised.

"You *know* this greaser?" Campbell pointed at the vaquero, now stirring weakly in the dirt.

"No, but that hardly matters, does it?" Slocum walked forward slowly. His cold eyes never left the drunken marshal. The slightest hint of movement for his six-shooter and Slocum would put a slug into the man's fat gut.

"Hell, maybe you just want to join in. Selfish of me not

to share the fun." Campbell turned to kick the Mexican again. In one smooth motion, Slocum drew and landed the barrel of his Colt alongside the marshal's head. George Campbell grunted and toppled like a tree felled by an expert lumberjack. The marshal lay sprawled on his back in the dust, arms outflung.

The vaquero moaned and got to his hands and knees. Slocum helped him to his feet. The man tried to struggle but the marshal's pistol-whipping and beating had robbed him of his strength.

"Come on. This town's going to get too hot for us in a few minutes." Slocum heard shouts going up from a tight knot of men in front of the Coliseum. They might not have seen or heard what happened in the street, but they had seen their marshal knocked flat.

The Mexican blinked and wiped blood from his forehead. "Those are the deputies," he said, pointing at two men fumbling for their six-shooters and starting down the street.

"And the rest of those men might be talked into forming a posse," Slocum said. "It's time for us to ride. You got a safe place where we can hole up?"

"Yes, yes, across the Rio Grande. They will not follow into Paso del Norte. They know better."

Slocum didn't ask how anyone as ignorant as Marshal Campbell could have learned such a lesson. Whoever had taught it must have a powerful grip on the Mexican side of the river. The shots echoing down the street convinced him he needed such a *patrón*'s protection.

He helped the vaquero around the Ben Dowell Saloon and to the stable. The boy hadn't got around to unsaddling Slocum's horse yet. For this bit of laziness Slocum was happy. Beside his black stallion was tethered a magnificently groomed roan. From the fancy tooling on the saddle, Slocum knew this horse belonged to the vaquero.

"Come on, *amigo*," he said. "We're going to have to ride for the border like we mean it."

"Why do you help me?" the vaquero asked suspiciously.

"Let's discuss that later, on the other side of the Rio Grande." Slocum drew his Colt Navy in a smooth motion and fired twice. The deputies yelped and dived for cover, giving Slocum time to mount. "Which way?"

The vaquero grinned broadly, his even, pearly white teeth showing in a dazzling grin. "What other way can there be, *amigo?* We ride south!"

Slocum spurred his nervous, bucking stallion after the vaquero as they wheeled about and headed south for the river and safety from the El Paso lawmen.

2

John Slocum ducked as a fusillade of bullets ripped through the air just above his head. He bent low over the stallion's neck and urged the powerful animal to even more speed. Froth began to form on the horse's flanks and its nostrils flared with every powerful breath. Only when they were safely out of El Paso did Slocum sit up in the saddle and begin reining back. Slowly, the black stallion eased its breakneck pace until it came to a halt.

Slocum waved to the vaquero. The Mexican rode his shiny-coated roan and tossed back his sombrero so that it hung by a leather thong around his neck and bounced lightly in the hot, dry wind blowing from the south.

"*Amigo,* I can only give my undying gratitude for your assistance. I am called Pedro Suarez."

"Since I seem to have worn out my welcome in El Paso, maybe you can help me over the border," said Slocum. He glanced over his shoulder to see if tiny dust clouds rose that might show a posse forming to come after him. He saw nothing suspicious. A single towering dust devil whipped upward over fifty feet into the air bouncing along the rocky desert and heading for a *bosque.* This was the only movement he saw in the area.

"My *patrón* will gladly see that you are rewarded."

Slocum thought on this a bit. The vaquero Pedro Suarez didn't look as if he worked for any *patrón.* The richness of

11

his clothing and the obvious breeding in the roan he rode told of real wealth. It hardly seemed likely a Mexican land owner would give such finery to a worker, even a valued foreman.

A new thought came to Slocum. Although he had never heard of such a thing, a wealthy *patrón* might outfit his valued men in such finery if the money meant nothing to him.

"I see what your thoughts are, *señor.*" Suarez smiled and winced. The marshal's beating had split the vaquero's lower lip and a trickle of blood started down his chin. Suarez rapidly wiped it away and spat. "My *patrón* is a generous and caring man." Suarez heaved a deep sigh. "And I am like the son he does not have."

"You rode into El Paso on his business?"

"No!" The sharpness of the answer told Slocum that he had poked into something that wasn't any of his business.

"Sorry," he said. "Didn't mean to pry, but it's pretty apparent that Marshal Campbell doesn't much cotton to Mexicans. You must have had powerful good reason to cross him."

"I have reason enough," Suarez said. The way he settled down in his hand-tooled saddle told Slocum there was no more to be gained from talk.

"I'd better be on my way. If I ride parallel to the Rio Grande and head through the pass, will that get me into New Mexico Territory?"

"But, *señor!*" Suarez protested. "You must come with me and accept the hospitality of my *patrón*. It is the least I can offer to such an unselfish man."

Slocum considered. Although there didn't seem to be any love lost between the marshal and the Texas Rangers, Slocum got the impression that either would be more than happy to string him up, especially if word came up from Van Horn that a Ranger had been gunned down. Any handy cowboy would do, but they'd like to settle more than one score, if possible. Pistol-whipping a marshal and gunning down a Texas Ranger sounded like a good pair of crimes to put together.

What worried Slocum the most was that he was responsible for both.

"How far is the Marsh Ranch?" he asked Suarez.

"Why do you ask? That is where the Rangers are quartered. You are not of their rank." Suarez eyed him closely. "You do not look like a lawman to me."

Slocum smiled grimly. "Just asking."

"They are four miles to the south and east. Those in El Paso welcomed them until they found how corrupt their captain was. Now they cannot get rid of them."

"A crooked Ranger captain and a drunken marshal. The people in El Paso have their troubles, don't they?"

"We will have none at the hacienda. Come, my friend, please. I owe you much. Let me repay it with the hospitality of my *patrón*. He will treat you as one of the family for your service to me this day."

"Not necessary," said Slocum, but he found himself liking Suarez and feeling increasingly curious about the man Suarez worked for. "But you make it sound attractive."

"For just one night. Then you can be on your way."

Slocum's stallion had regained some of its strength. He urged the horse to the south until they came to the banks of the Rio Grande. Spring runoff had begun higher up in the Rockies, near the Colorado border, and turned the river into a raging ribbon of muddy brown water too dangerous to ford.

"There is a shallow near Zaragosa," Suarez said. "It takes us out of the way, but it is the only good crossing this time of year."

Slocum followed. The ride took them several miles down river in the direction of Ysleta. Slocum recognized the ford immediately; it would still prove a dangerous crossing. He started down the bank.

"*Señor*, no! Wait. We cross here, yes, but on a barge.

The river is more than twenty feet deep, even at this shallow point."

Slocum frowned. He saw the telltale vee marks in the swiftly flowing river, betraying hidden sandbars. When the flat-bottomed barge hove into view, though, he saw the wisdom of using it to get to the other side of the Rio Grande. They led their horses onto the barge. Pedro Suarez spoke rapidly to the men lined up on either side of the barge and coins changed hands. They moved out and were caught up in the flow.

Even if the river had been shallow enough to cross, the current would have swept his horse off its feet, Slocum saw. When they crossed over the sandbars, he peered down into the murky water. The sand shifted ominously even as he watched. The sudden drop-offs on either side hid the true depth.

"The Rio Grande is a most treacherous river, *señor*," Pedro said, seeing his interest. "For most of the year, you can walk across and never get your boots damp. But in the spring . . ." He pointed to the effect of the melting snow high in the mountains.

It took over an hour to get safely to the other side. Slocum felt better about pursuit. Let the drunken George Campbell come after him. The man would drown crossing the river.

"How far to the hacienda?" he asked Pedro.

"*Señor,* we are already on the land of my *patrón*. As far as you can see, it is his land. To the hacienda is but an hour's ride."

Slocum studied the terrain as they rode. It was as barren as any he had crossed coming from the Hueco Mountains and into El Paso, but everywhere he looked fat cattle chewed contentedly at the sparse grass. His quick mind made the count. Pedro Suarez's boss might own as many as ten thousand head of cattle. That made him more than rich. It made him richer than Slocum's dreams of avarice.

"There," said Pedro. "Is she not a beautiful place?"

The design of the hacienda copied any of a thousand other Spanish dwellings Slocum had seen, but the hints of wealth abounded. The outer walls of the compound were plain adobe. The gates were fine mahogany and intricately carved.

"Where did the wood come from?" he asked.

"Los índios brought it up from the interior," came the simple answer.

Slocum didn't ask how many Indian slaves had died bringing the lustrous wood from Central Mexico on their backs. The early Spanish priests had killed thousands bringing wood *vígas* from Yucatan simply to support the roofs of their churches. The Indian blood had only made the churches more sacred in the priests' minds. To Slocum it turned the rich cathedrals into gold-leafed mortuaries.

"Pedro! You are back!" came a voice that Slocum found hauntingly familiar. From a side door lumbered a portly man, a brightly embroidered sash around his middle. Calf-high black leather boots had white cotton trousers tucked in the tops. The shirt was woven with gold threads and far too gaudy for Slocum's tastes.

But then, he and Don Ynocente Ochoa had not shared the same taste in clothing, even if they had taken a liking to the same cattle.

"Patrón! I have failed to find her."

"You are injured," Don Ynocente said, his voice hard. "Who did this to you? Was it Doc Manning?"

"No, *patrón,* but this does not matter. This man helped me to escape. But I did not find Consuela."

Don Ynocente looked past Pedro for the first time. His eyes held Slocum, then narrowed as he tried to remember. A slow smile crossed his lips.

"This is the man who helped you? This *pendejo?* This *jóta?"*

Pedro's eyebrows shot up and almost vanished beneath his sombrero. "He fought their marshal. He kept me from a severe beating. No one, not even you, can speak of him in such a way!"

"Pedro, don't worry," Slocum said. "I know all about Don Ynocente. Never have I seen a sneakier, more low-down son-of-a-bitch cow rustler. He'd steal your last nickel and then complain if he had to shoot you because he couldn't afford the slug."

"You, you two know each other?" Pedro finally understood that their words carried no true insult.

Slocum slipped from the saddle and landed heavily. He found himself caught up in a bear hug as Don Ynocente threw his arms around him.

"Slocum, it has been such a long time."

"When was it? Five years ago? Eight?"

"More!" cried Don Ynocente. "Do you not remember the cold nights in Laredo these fourteen years ago?"

"I remember the cold nights. Damn, but rustling those cows was hard work."

"And when we drove them over the border, we only got two dollars a head for them because the buyer knew they were stolen," the Mexican remembered.

"That was because of your sloppy branding. The real brand was still visible. You never could run a brand worth shit."

"No, no, it was because— But wait, why do we talk outside in the hottest part of the day? Let us go into the courtyard where it is cool and we can drink!"

Slocum wasn't about to argue, even though the sun had set and the desert winds had turned chilly. In another hour, the wind would be downright cold. He followed Don Ynocente inside through the corridor that led into a garden area. The rooms of the hacienda protected this inner courtyard on all four sides, making it a refuge from the harsh outer world.

"Pedro, bring us tequila." Don Ynocente paused for a moment, then added in a more subdued tone, "For the three of us. We must discuss this matter fully."

"Sí, patrón, right away."

To Slocum, Ynocente Ochoa said, "Come and sit. Make yourself at home. But then, you always did. Now I have a home to offer in way of hospitality."

"You've done well," Slocum said, easing into a chair made from woven strips of tanned cowhide. "All this from rustling? Or did you find another way of making yourself rich?"

"The rustling, yes, those were interesting days," Don Ynocente said, lost in memories of the time spent with Slocum in South Texas many years ago. "I have used my money and influence well. I am now a prominent *patrón.*"

"What of Don Juan? Your brother was always more ambitious than you were."

"Some things do not change. Juan is now *jéfe político* of Paso del Norte."

Slocum accepted the tequila from a tray held by Pedro. Ynocente's brother being the head of government in Paso del Norte made the entire Ochoa family immensely powerful. The obvious wealth no longer surprised Slocum. Juan controlled the army and Don Ynocente had gone from rustling cattle to collecting taxes.

He wasn't sure that the cattle stealing wasn't the more honorable profession.

He looked from Ynocente's composed features to Pedro's more agitated expression. Ynocente's reaction meant nothing. Slocum had learned too many years ago that he couldn't play poker with Ynocente; the man betrayed nothing in his face. Pedro's response meant much more.

"If Don Juan is so powerful in border politics, why send Pedro into El Paso alone?'

"You never appreciated the uniquely Spanish art of conversation, of *habladuría.*"

"When I have something to say, I say it. Otherwise, why beat around the bush? Life's too damned short to waste on your *habladuría,* on idle chatter."

"You understand us better than you let on," said Don Ynocente. "It is just that you do not accept our ways."

"I accept them, but I don't embrace them," said Slocum. "I reckon a man can believe any damn thing he wants. That's his business. But it doesn't mean I have to believe it, too."

"Please, *Señor* Slocum, you must help me. I have been unable to find her." Pedro dropped to his knees as if praying. He still clutched the tray with the tequila bottle on it. Slocum poured himself another shot and tried to ignore the man's groveling.

"Pedro," Don Ynocente said irritably, "this is none of Slocum's business. This is a family matter."

"You don't consider me part of the family any longer, Ynocente?" asked Slocum. "That wasn't what you said when I saved Juan from that lynch mob in Corpus Christi."

Even as the words left his mouth, Slocum knew that Ynocente had maneuvered him into a dangerous position. Slocum had indirectly volunteered to help in whatever way he could, and Slocum had no idea what he was getting himself into. He silently cursed himself for being so rash and Ynocente for being so subtle.

"The situation across the border is unsettled," Ynocente said in his roundabout fashion. Slocum knew he would get to the problem in his own time. "El Paso is ravaged by bands of roving criminals."

"They are even more ravaged by their own lawmen," said Slocum. "Marshal Campbell was beating up on Pedro something fierce when I stopped him."

"Campbell is not dangerous," said Ynocente Ochoa. "The captain of Texas Rangers, this Captain Baylor, is. But even these corrupt men pose few problems for those on this side of the Rio Grande."

"What took Pedro into El Paso?" asked Slocum. "You must have had enough other vaqueros to send along to help him."

"We have several hundred workers on the hacienda,"

Ynocente said. "If my brother Don Juan sees fit, we can send a thousand or more armed soldiers into El Paso, but this will not necessarily get our little dove back."

Slocum stayed quiet. He might have known a woman would be at the center of the problem. Ynocente Ochoa had always had a roving eye, even when they were in the middle of a desolate wasteland. Slocum smiled slowly, remembering how Ynocente had taken up with the Yaqui squaw and had provoked the entire tribe to come hunting for them.

"She is . . . Pedro's daughter," Ynocente said. Slocum's attention snapped back to the *patrón*. Something in the way the man spoke alerted Slocum. She might be Pedro Suarez's daughter but there was more. What? Ynocente Ochoa did not say.

"She was kidnapped?" Slocum asked.

"*Sí*, yes, she was!" blurted Pedro. "One night I go to her room and she is not there. There is no sign of her."

"I sent a dozen of my best vaqueros to find her trail," said Ynocente. "It led north, across the Rio Grande. She has been missing for three days and nights now."

Slocum waited for Ynocente to continue. When he did not, Slocum knew Ynocente was hiding important parts from him.

"For her, I will devote my life," said Ynocente. "She is like a daughter to me, although she is of Pedro's loins." Ynocente Ochoa downed a shot of tequila and took another, staring into the clear liquor as if he could find the vanished girl there. "I have no sons, Slocum. Pedro will become *patrón* when I die."

This shocked Slocum, although Pedro had hinted at something similar earlier. Most Mexicans would pass their property along to a brother or a brother's son rather than deed it over to someone outside the family. That Ynocente lacked a male heir startled Slocum even more. The man's profligate ways should have made half the young men in the country his bastard heirs.

"I will do anything to get Consuela back where she belongs, Slocum," Don Ynocente said. "I allowed Pedro to seek her on his own. He is her father; it was his duty. But I cannot send an army across the river, as much as I want to."

"The Texas Rangers?" Slocum asked.

"In part. Captain Baylor is not an easy man to reason with. The Manning brothers are crooks and control much of El Paso. The Mannings and the Ochoas have not seen eye to eye on political matters, if you understand my meaning."

Slocum did. Two powerful families battling for dominance built up powerful emotions—anger and fear.

"If the Mannings are responsible for stealing away Consuela, I will not rest until they are all dead," Ynocente finished.

"Do they understand that this might spark a blood feud?" asked Slocum.

"They are arrogant gringos. What do they care? I must know for certain if they have kidnapped Consuela."

Slocum's belly turned to ice. Ynocente spoke for Pedro Suarez's benefit. Don Ynocente seemed to know Consuela's fate, and that it had nothing to do with the Manning family kidnapping her. If it had, he would never have been this reluctant to mount an expedition across the Rio Grande to retrieve her.

"We must proceed cautiously, for the girl's life is at stake. There is much more to consider."

Slocum nodded. Ynocente Ochoa truly wanted the return of the girl. Sincerity rang in his words. And for his own reasons, he did not want to anger the Manning family needlessly. Pedro Suarez had tried to find his daughter in El Paso and had failed. Slocum worried over what lurked just beneath the surface of these few facts Ynocente had revealed.

"If you describe her, maybe I can return her," Slocum said. The words burned his tongue as he spoke. Marshal George Campbell wanted him dead. Texas Rangers sought someone—him—for killing a Ranger down Van Horn way. The El Paso marshal wanted his blood, and he was volunteering to find Consuela Suarez.

Slocum wondered if he hadn't been in the hot spring-time sun too long. When he saw the look of triumph on Ynocente Ochoa's face, he knew he had again been lured into doing the *patrón*'s dirty work.

3

John Slocum tossed and turned all night in the too-soft bed. Feather pillows and a mattress fleecier than a white, puffy cloud had been all too rare in his life lately. He had become accustomed to sleeping under the stars, a thin blanket pulled up around his shoulders to hold back the cold desert night winds. This luxury took getting used to.

Slocum rose from the bed, stretched, and went to the door opening into the central courtyard. Insects whirred through the night and a hunting bat swooped down, made a quick scouting trip in its vigilant search for juicy insects, then wheeled around, chittered, and vanished. Slocum went into the cool courtyard and stood staring upward at the clear, diamond-hard points of the stars.

"They seem close enough to touch, do they not?" came Don Ynocente Ochoa's soft voice.

Slocum turned to his right. The man sat in a chair, hidden in deep shadows, as quiet and unmoving as if he were the hunter waiting for his prey.

"I couldn't sleep. Damned bed's too soft."

"Too lonely, perhaps, *amigo?*" asked Ynocente, joking. "I might find a maid who is willing to share the comforts and pleasures of your bed. Maria was overheard speaking of you to another in the kitchen. She thinks you are very *guapo.*"

"And I am sure Maria is very *bonita,*" Slocum responded. He found a chair and sat down so that he faced Don Ynocente. Neither man could be seen easily by the other, owing to the way the shadows were cast. Slocum decided that Ynocente wanted it this way.

Was the man's poker face showing emotion this night? What upset him so? Slocum knew it had to be more than his foreman's daughter being kidnapped by the Manning brothers.

"Tell me about Consuela."

"So beautiful, so headstrong. A fine girl."

"This fine girl wasn't kidnapped, was she?"

For several minutes Ynocente did not speak. He gusted a sigh and finally said, "No. I did not trust my hunters to follow her trail. She is very clever and I have taught her all she knows."

"But not all *you* know, Don Ynocente." Slocum made it a flat statement. It startled him that Ynocente admitted to sharing any of his considerable tracking knowledge with a woman. Ynocente's Spanish heritage divided women into two categories—whores and good girls. Good girls did not learn such skills.

"No. I trailed her to the river. She went of her own volition. No one accompanied her."

"You are sure she is in El Paso?"

"Somewhere near. Find her for me, John. Bring her home where she belongs. El Paso is no fit place for anyone these days. I allowed Pedro to seek her there only because he is her father and it is his duty, but I knew he would not locate her. She is far too clever for him."

"I'll be gone by sunup." Slocum waited for Ynocente's answer. When it did not come, Slocum rose and went to the chair where the *patrón* had sat. The cowhide strips still carried the imprint left by his heavy body but of the man Slocum saw nothing. Ynocente Ochoa had not lost any of his skill.

Slocum returned to his room and lay on his back, staring at the exposed wood beams in the ceiling and thinking.

Both Juan and Ynocente had been his friends long ago when they rustled cattle around Laredo, and each had saved the other's life too many times to count. Slocum just wished he knew what he was getting himself involved in.

Sleep came but his dreams were not easy. Posses chased him. Texas Rangers shot at him. And marshals dropped nooses over his head before swatting the sturdy rump of his stallion, to leave him dangling by his neck.

Getting back across the Rio Grande proved harder than getting into Mexico. The barge had sunk during the night, after hitting a rock in the center of the river. Two of the crew and the owner had drowned in the swift current. Slocum decided it might be for the best that he went farther upriver, toward New Mexico Territory, and found a ford. It took the better part of a day getting across the river, and he couldn't help wondering if he had ever left Ynocente Ochoa's land until he returned to Texas.

He crossed the Southern Pacific Railroad tracks and followed them to the depot five miles to the west of central El Paso. Slocum wasn't sure where to begin his search. Don Ynocente had not been specific about the places Consuela might have sought out, but Slocum had been able to come to his own conclusions.

Don Ynocente thought of Consuela Suarez as a nice girl. This prevented the man from reaching the inescapable conclusion about her. Slocum had inquired of the stablehands at the hacienda and had got only stony stares for an answer. He had not expected more. But he needed a name —the name of the man Consuela had run away to meet.

The sun hung low in the west. He shook his head. An entire day had been wasted getting across the Rio Grande. Two days had passed since he had ridden into El Paso. And what did he have to show for it? Marshal Campbell would be out for blood. He was on a mission for a man the Manning brothers hated, and they seemed to be the power in El Paso. Slocum knew the smartest thing he could do was buy a ticket on the first westbound train and lose himself in Arizona or California.

Instead, he went to the ticket agent and asked, "I'm looking for a friend of mine. Think he's got himself into a bit of trouble."

"Trouble's not hard to find in these parts," said the wizened man in the barred booth.

"Didn't anyone come looking for a train to the west with a Mexican girl in tow, was there?"

"What'd he look like? What'd *she* look like?"

Slocum knew that the agent would have remembered. Ynocente's description of Consuela made her out to be the most gorgeous woman who had ever walked the face of the earth. Slocum guessed that she was pretty, but not as lovely as Ynocente said. But the agent would remember. How many Mexican women—ladies—accompanied a gringo?

"Reckon they didn't come this way."

"Don't see that combination much," the ticket agent admitted. "I'd be inclined to remember if they had." The man thought a minute, then said, "Did see one of them small people last month. What do you call them? Midgets. That's it. A midget came through on his way to join up with Molly Bailey's circus over in Houston."

Slocum had no interest in midgets. He turned and went to the station platform. Consuela might have tried riding the rails or hiding in a freight car, but he doubted it. Such a desperate act would never occur to a properly reared Spanish lady. She might talk about it as romantic, but she would never do it.

That left Slocum with the unpleasant notion that she was holed up somewhere in El Paso.

He didn't have the slightest idea how to find her without causing interest in his questions among people he wanted to avoid.

Slocum rode the five miles into El Paso, wary of riders passing him on the road. None paid him any heed. By the time he reached the center of town, he began to wonder if the hue and cry had been put out for him at all. Feeling reckless, he rode around to the stable behind the Ben Dowell Saloon and dismounted. The same stableboy slept behind a bale of hay. Slocum didn't bother him. Having his stallion ready for the road would be a boon, should he have to leave quickly again.

Slocum entered the side door of the saloon. Sundown had come and the saloon patrons had come out in droves. The bartender worked hard just to keep the tequila and beer in front of his thirsty customers. Jake worked so hard that his mustache tips had drooped and he had not taken the time to wax them into stiff points.

Slocum leaned against the bar. Jake's eyes widened but the man said nothing more than, "The usual?"

Slocum nodded. When the barkeep put the shot and beer in front of him, he said in a low voice, "You're a damned fool to come back like this. Unless you figured it out for yourself."

"What's that?" Slocum downed the tequila and chased it with a long draught of beer.

"Campbell was so damned drunk he don't remember nothing. He woke up with a headache and his guts heaving, but he don't even remember the Mexican. Nobody else saw you. Leastways, not enough to identify you proper. You're one lucky hombre."

"You saw me," Slocum pointed out.

"I don't see nothing, except when a thirsty man's glass is empty."

Slocum gestured for the barkeep to set up another round. Jake had confirmed what he had suspected. George Campbell had been so far in his cups that everything had blacked out, including the marshal's memory. Slocum watched with apprehension, though, when Marshal Campbell came through the swinging doors.

The lawman looked neither left nor right. He plowed through the crowd like a charging bull buffalo and headed for a table at the rear of the saloon where three men sat playing poker.

Jake drifted back, sweat beading his forehead. "You're a damned lucky one. He never even glanced this way. Went straight back to talk with the boss."

"Who's that?"

"Frank Manning. That's him in the brown coat. His brother Doc's the one with the beard and the scowl. The other one's Johnny Hale, a friend of theirs—the one who looks like he can eat corn on the cob through a picket fence."

Slocum couldn't believe his ears. He had stumbled into the saloon owned by the very men Ynocente Ochoa fought with across the border.

"Where would a man find a place to stay for the night —a nice place, not a whorehouse."

"Hard to name in El Paso," Jake said, scratching his head. "You might consider the Central Hotel. Been a gaggle of highfalutin people stayin' there," said Jake. "When the AT&SF came down from Lamy, even Don Espiridon Provencio from down in Mexico City stayed there for the celebration."

Slocum finished the tequila and left the saloon. Jake had told him all he needed to know. If Consuela had to choose a place in El Paso, the Central Hotel would be it. The idea that a high-ranking representative of her government had stayed at the hotel would make it the only decent place for her to consider.

Slocum wandered along Mesa Avenue until he came to Texas Street. The Central Hotel rose up three stories, the tallest building in sight. He went inside and felt out of place because of the way he was dressed. He wondered if a menial would come along behind and clean the dusty footprints he left from the posh rug. The clerk appeared not to notice Slocum's dishevelment.

"I'm looking for a woman," Slocum said. The clerk's watery blue eyes turned to ice. "Not like that," Slocum corrected. The clerk's attitude did not soften. "Her name's Consuela Suarez. Her father's sent me to look for her."

"The young woman to whom you refer has been evicted," the clerk said primly, ignoring Slocum by turning back to his pointless leafing through registration cards.

"How long has she been gone? Where did she go?"

"This morning," the clerk said, "we seized her luggage as partial payment of her room. She and the . . . gentleman with her attempted to leave without paying."

"How much was the bill?" Slocum asked. For the first time he had the clerk's undivided attention.

"Rooms are four-fifty a night. They . . . stayed for three nights."

Slocum silently pulled a twenty-dollar gold piece from his pocket and dropped it on the counter. It rang musically, rolled around, then settled down.

The clerk licked his lips. "The luggage is in storage. This way, please." Slocum followed the clerk to a small closet where Consuela's luggage had been stacked. Slocum shook his head in amazement. For a girl running away from home to be with her boyfriend, Consuela had managed to take enough to outfit a dozen women.

"I'll get your change," the clerk said when Slocum was laden down with the three bulky suitcases.

"Tell me where she is now and you can keep the change," Slocum said.

"I . . . I don't know. You might try the church. The Church of St. Clements, between Mills and Texas."

Slocum dragged the luggage from the hotel lobby and lashed it behind his saddle. His stallion protested the awkward load. Slocum walked his horse down the street until he came to the church.

He didn't have to enter. At the rear a man and a woman stood arguing loudly. From Don Ynocente's description, the woman could be no one but Consuela Suarez. She was dressed in an intricately patterned skirt and ruffled white linen blouse embroidered with red and green figures of parrots. Beneath the hem of the skirt Slocum saw soft leather riding boots. Everything about her proclaimed wealth.

She swore a blue streak in Spanish that the man couldn't follow. Slocum smiled. Don Ynocente's perfect lady knew more than she had ever let on.

"You lowdown, no-account son of a *beetch!*" she shouted in English. "What do you mean there is another?"

"Consuela, listen, calm down, please!" the man with her pleaded.

"You do not pay the hotel bill. You try to sneak off and not tell me. Now, when I find you, you say there is another! I should rip out your eyes!"

"*Señorita* Suarez," Slocum said softly.

Both Consuela and her boyfriend turned. Slocum's hand moved slightly, getting into a better position to draw his Colt. The other man's expression turned ugly and his hand twitched just above the butt of his pistol.

"Who the hell are you?" the man bellowed. "Leave us be. This is none of your concern."

"*Señorita*, your father and Don Ynocente are worried about you. They want you to come home. I'm John Slocum. They sent me for you."

"I seen you somewhere," the man said, his eyes narrowing.

"You're wrong about that, *amigo*," Slocum said. "Consuela, I have your luggage. Let's go home."

"You're the son of a bitch what beat on Marshal Campbell yesterday."

"He did this thing?" Consuela asked, her eyes wide. Slocum tried to figure out what her expression meant. She showed no fear. If anything, there was a hint of excitement about her. Animal excitement.

"The marshal was having at your father. I stopped him."

"You *are* the son of a bitch!"

The man's hand worked to get his six-shooter free. Slocum's reflexes were faster. His fist drove hard into the man's chin. The man grunted and fell to one knee, still trying to get his gun free of his holster.

Consuela saved the man's life. She struggled with him and knocked his pistol into the dust.

"Reach for it and you're buzzard bait," Slocum said. His rock-steady aim convinced the man.

"You are a gunfighter?" Consuela asked. Again Slocum got the feel of excitement in her.

"Just doing a favor for a friend. You got a horse? Get on. We're going back to Mexico. Right now."

"Luke is a deputy marshal," Consuela said, obviously enjoying the revelation. "He is a dangerous man, and you have reduced him to a nothing!"

Slocum considered putting a slug between the deputy's eyes. That would make everything easier.

"Go mount up," Slocum ordered.

"You will shoot him down like the dog he is?"

Slocum's cold stare caused Consuela to scurry off. He turned back to the deputy.

"Go on, murder me, you—" The deputy's words cut off abruptly when Slocum smashed the barrel of his Colt alongside the man's head. Slocum didn't like doing this. The front sight always came loose and too many impacts like this loosened the cylinder. He would have to strip the six-shooter and completely rework it.

The deputy lay on his side in the dust. Again Slocum wondered if he should kill the man. If he didn't, there would be a posse after them soon.

"You will kill him for me," Consuela ordered. "Now. Kill him now!"

That decided Slocum. He lowered the Colt's hammer and stuck it back into his holster. "I hope you're ready to ride, because we're not stopping until we get back to Don Ynocente's hacienda."

"But Luke. You . . . I ordered you to kill him!"

Slocum grabbed the reins of the willful woman's horse and jerked the animal's head around. He wished it were

Consuela Suarez wearing the bridle and bit. Maybe then he could get her attention and make her understand that he wasn't anyone's hired killer. Not hers, not Don Ynocente's, no one's.

4

Slocum turned when Consuela Suarez drew even with him. He pulled down the brim of his hat to shield his eyes from the sun hanging low in the west. She rode like a man, he decided, but after that conclusion any confusion about her sex ended. Long black hair so dark that it carried blue highlights flowed behind as she rode. Her beauty made him ache, and she knew it. Consuela pulled back her shoulders and thrust out her chest. Slocum wondered if the elaborately decorated ruffled blouse might tear with the pressure her breasts put on it. Somehow the cloth held. And so did his self-control.

"Señor," she said, her voice soft and lilting, "why do you come for me like this? I thank you for getting me away from that . . . *that.*" She sputtered incoherently, switched to Spanish, then returned to English. "Thank you for what you have done."

"How did you get involved with that man?" Slocum asked. As they rode, he forced himself to look around. Luke might be recovering his senses by now. His reaction to all that had happened worried Slocum. A deputy marshal might fetch a posse or a lynch mob. Even though Consuela rode well, Slocum knew they could never reach the Rio Grande and cross its spring swelling before the law would catch them.

"Luke . . . excited me. I met him when my *dueña* and I

came to El Paso seeking out a certain linen brought in on the train from San Francisco."

"You met him and him being a deputy made you respect him."

"Respect? For that pig? Never. He is an animal. *That* is what excited me." Consuela batted her long black eyelashes at Slocum and asked in a sultry voice, "Are you an animal, too?"

"Can't say the idea ever came to me." Slocum kept his voice level but he remembered back to the days when he had ridden with Quantrill's Raiders. He and Quantrill and Bloody Bill Anderson and the rest had been worse than animals. They had slaughtered, some for the sick thrill of it, others like Slocum because they thought it was their duty as soldiers for the Confederacy. He had been wrong and when he'd complained about the Lawrenceville massacre of innocent women and children, they'd gutshot him and left him for dead.

They had been animals. Were they what Consuela Suarez sought in a man? He glanced at the young woman again. Her cheeks carried a light rosy flush of excitement. She held her head high and haughty and rode easily. Slocum guessed it was the danger of the relationship that thrilled her. Slocum knew how the Mexican men protected their women. Consuela was proud and intelligent and beautiful. She had to feel she was a prisoner on the restrictive hacienda and sought a break in the deadly dull routine.

Slocum hoped it was nothing more than that.

"Tell me about Luke. Is he likely to come after us?"

"Luke?" Consuela laughed. "He talks the bigness but he walks like a mouse. No, he would go tell his brothers. Only with all the Mannings behind him would Luke again be the real man he thinks he is."

"Luke Manning? His brothers are Doc and Frank?"

"You know them." Consuela seemed not to have a care in the world. Slocum closed his eyes for a moment and tried to think as the wind whipped in his face and the powerful stallion worked to put distance between Luke Manning and Slocum.

No matter how hard and fast they rode, they would never be able to avoid the Mannings. From what Don Ynocente said, they owned El Paso. Having their brother humiliated by the daughter of Ochoa's foreman would be too great a shame to bear. Only blood would retrieve the deputy's lost honor.

Slocum reined in and motioned for Consuela to stop, too. "What is it?" she asked. "Why do we not ride back to my prison on the hacienda? Do you wish to run off with me? We can be on the train and bound for Lamy within an hour."

Slocum said nothing to her proposal. He had seriously considered getting on the next train—alone. Consuela was a lightning rod for danger. As long as they rode together, he was in big trouble. Then Slocum smiled ruefully. Consuela didn't add that much to his worries when the Texas Rangers still sought a killer. What was another tidbit of trouble?

Slocum sobered. He could never go back on his word to Ynocente. He had promised to return Consuela to the hacienda, and he would. It was just proving more difficult than he had anticipated.

"We can't get across the border before the Mannings come for us, so we're going to cut back in that direction."

"Toward the mountains?" Consuela frowned. Slocum thought even this looked pretty. "But the Franklins are so rugged. There is no water there. Only a few foolish tin miners go there."

"Would Luke ever think you'd head in that direction?"

"No, never."

Slocum wheeled his stallion and started off.

"Wait!" Consuela cried. "You cannot leave me like this."

"Then you'd better ride in the same direction I'm heading." Slocum chose a path that wound around, not so much to confuse the deputy if he tracked them but to get his own bearings. The outskirts of El Paso were dotted with small, well-kept, flat-roofed adobe houses. Big-eyed children watched as he and Consuela rode past. Slocum corrected that: They watched Consuela. Most had seen gunmen before. Few had seen such an obviously wealthy lady in their midst.

"Why do we ride in this direction?" Consuela asked, her voice edged with steely disapproval. "There is only Fort Bliss and the filthy dog soldiers there."

"We're bypassing the fort," Slocum said. He had the lay of the land well in mind now. They rode to the north of central El Paso and found a dirt road winding through the desert and leading into the foothills of the Franklins. Heavy wagons had come along this road recently, he noted. Consuela had mentioned tin mines. Squinting into the setting sun he thought he saw gleaming, raw rock tailings falling out from small shafts bored straight into hard mountain rock. He wanted to avoid those, if possible. When the marshal came hunting for them, he didn't want tongues flapping about the lovely Mexican *señorita* and the hard-looking man with her.

"What will we do when darkness is complete?" asked Consuela in a testy voice. "I do not like being outside like this. The desert wind is cold and sleeping on hard rock with rattlesnakes is below my station."

Slocum wondered what her station was. It shouldn't be all that high if she were the daughter of Pedro Suarez. What status was given to the daughter of a ranch foreman? Not much down in Mexico, Slocum knew. Consuela had to be something more. Ynocente had always been something of a rake. Slocum wondered if the don had taken this fiery young woman as his mistress. He wouldn't put it past Ynocente, and it explained his distress at having her leave to be with Luke Maning.

"You can go back into El Paso if you want," Slocum said.

"Very well." Consuela tossed her head back like a high-spirited filly, as if daring him to argue.

"I doubt if Luke and his brothers will take kindly to you after what I did. Fact is, they might blame you."

"Luke would never do such a thing."

"You called him some pretty vile names. And you said he was an animal. Don't want to think much on what happens when a wild animal gets out of its pen after it's been poked and made fun of. Give Don Ynocente my regards."

"Wait, Slocum. Very well. I will stay with you this night. If you can provide suitable accommodations, that is."

"We'll see what we can find." Slocum turned off the road and let his stallion pick the way through the prairie dog and snake holes. The sand was cooling off and the twilight hunting time had begun. Slocum saw jackrabbits timidly feeding and a coyote boldly hunting. Slocum felt a kinship with the life stirring from their rest. He came alive this time of day. Life stirred everywhere, some dangerous, some not, all interesting.

"I am growing tired. We must stop." Consuela had turned from testy to irritable. Slocum ignored her and kept riding. He had found a small canyon leading into the mountains with a deserted, overgrown double-rutted road giving promise of abandoned buildings. Ten minutes' ride delivered on that faint promise.

"There," he said. "A roof over our head for the night."

"That?" Consuela shrieked. "That is an old mining shack. It is not fit for rats!"

"It's not the Central Hotel, but then the room rates are more reasonable." Slocum dismounted and began tending his horse. The stallion had done well by him and he wanted to give the animal all the rest possible. Small clumps of dry grass grew nearby. Slocum let the horse work on those while he fetched water from a pump with a leather sucker-washer cracked almost beyond use. Ten minutes' hard work and a spot of luck brought up a brown flow of water.

Another few minutes' pumping produced clear, clean water. Slocum sampled it and made a face. Too much iron in it, but the water still tasted better than any fine Kentucky whiskey he'd ever sipped. Riding all day in the hot springtime desert had dried him out more than he'd thought.

To his surprise Consuela had not waited, thinking he would take care of her horse. She had wiped the animal down and had led it to graze beside his stallion.

Consuela looked up, her dark eyes flashing. "You will inspect this miserable shack first. I do not wish to disturb the rats."

"The desert rats seemed to have left," Slocum said. He kicked open the stubbornly resisting door and almost knocked it from its rusty hinges. Inside he found only what he'd expected. A table lacked one leg. A cot along the back wall had been stripped of blankets and whatever mattress that had once rested on it. A small three-legged stool had been overturned and left beside the slanting table. A spot where an iron stove had once stood showed only charred markings of feet; the previous owner had taken the valuable stove with him. The shack would get mighty cold during the night without it.

"This will give us some protection from the wind," said Slocum. He dropped his bedroll onto the floor beside the cot. Without a pad on the cot, he knew the floor would be more comfortable.

"This is all? You are going to sleep here? Where do you expect me to sleep?"

"There's plenty of room," Slocum pointed out. "We might knock a hole in the floor and build a small fire where the stove used to be since the flue pipe is still in place. That leaves a spot over here for you." He drew imaginary boxes in the air to show Consuela where she could sleep.

"You will do the cooking?" Consuela cocked her head to one side and stared at him with growing suspicion. "There *is* food?"

"Trail rations," Slocum said. "They'll keep us from

starving." Slocum baited the woman. He had better than
dry trial rations. Don Ynocente had given him enough food
to last a week or more and dine in style the entire time.

Consuela sat on the low stool and watched as he kicked
out the rotted wood floor and placed rocks around the
crude fireplace. Using part of the wood from the floor, he
started a fire. Mesquite and dried cholla provided a fragrant
smoke and an agreeable warmth. He fixed a supper far
better than he had let on. Consuela ate hungrily and asked
for another helping.

"You are very good at this," she said. "I cannot cook.
There is no reason for me to learn."

"Reckon not, with a hacienda filled with servants. If I
never learned, I'd've starved to death a long time ago."

"You are what they call a drifter?"

At this Slocum only nodded. Settling down had never
appealed much to him. He looked at Consuela and idly
wondered what it would be like living with a woman so
beautiful and headstrong.

"You are not being paid, are you?" she asked suddenly.

"No. Why do you ask?"

"You come for me as a favor to Don Ynocente. You said
so. I do not often find an honorable man, or one so brave."

"Damned stupid, if you ask me. I should have killed
Luke Manning."

"But you could not because he was unconscious. You
are brave, honorable, and have a kind heart." She dropped
to her knees on the edge of his blanket. A long-fingered
hand reached out and gently touched his cheek. "You are
also strong and very handsome."

Slocum bent forward when Consuela closed her dark
eyes. His lips found her full, moist ones. They kissed. Her
lips parted and the tip of a questing pink tongue sought out
his. Slocum's heart felt as if it would explode and his groin
turned to fire. He clutched the woman to him as if she
might try to run away.

There was no danger of that. Her fingers struggled to

pull open her blouse and expose golden brown breasts, each capped with a darker brown nipple. Slocum's hands stroked up along Consuela's flat belly and came to rest on those firm, warm mounds. His hands squeezed, gently at first, then with more insistence as Consuela moaned and sobbed and shoved herself against him.

They sank down to the padding offered by the thin blankets. Neither noticed the hardness of the floor. They were too engrossed with exploring each other's bodies.

"Oh, John, you are so strong," Consuela gasped when she managed to unfasten both Slocum's gun belt and his denims. Her fingers curled around his hard shaft. "Take me now, John. I need *this* within me." She gripped his stiff, straining manhood so tightly that he thought he would explode.

He slipped over on top of her, the woman's legs parting wantonly for him. He eased forward, spearing her and lifting the woman off the floor.

She clung to him, her fingers raking along his back. Slocum hardly noticed. He bent forward and kissed her. Still buried to the hilt within her, he worked down, kissing throat and ear and lips again and each breast. The nipples pulsed with every frenzied beat of her heart. He felt it all through his lips and tongue.

"Move, John. Do not torment me so!"

He eased back, hating to leave the tight sheath surrounding his turgid length. When only the tip of his rock-hard length remained inside, he paused, then stroked back in smoothly. This brought another gasp of joy from Consuela's quivering lips. She clung to him, tears forming at the corners of her eyes.

"You are so good, so very, very good," she sobbed out. "I was such a fool to be with Luke. I missed so much by not being with you! More, John, give me more!"

Slocum cut off further words with his mouth. He kissed and bit and tongued her lips and ears even as his hips levered back and forth. Each stroke forced him to exert a bit more self-control. She crushed down around him and squeezed with such carnal pleasure that he thought he was going to erupt at any instant.

He wanted to make this last as long as possible, but Consuela's demanding body robbed him of mastery. He lost himself in a heady mixture of sweat and lust. He began thrusting harder and harder, the friction burning them both and sending their desires to new heights. Consuela was past words. She groaned and began shoving her crotch up to meet his every inward stroke.

Locked together, they gasped in unison. Slocum arched his back in a vain attempt to penetrate even deeper into the woman's body. His length exploded within her, his hips went wild, and he lost all control over the rhythm of his lovemaking.

Panting, he sagged down atop her. Consuela's face and shoulders were flushed into a golden hue. She opened her eyes. It took several seconds for her to focus.

"You are good, very good," she said.

"It's been a spell."

"For one as good as you, that should not happen. Let us make sure you do not wait so long again." Her knowing fingers found the flaccid length dangling between his legs. In minutes she had coaxed life into it again.

Slocum knew that he should not be making love to a woman under Don Ynocente's protection. A woman who must be the powerful man's mistress. He shouldn't.

But he did. Again.

5

Slocum rolled over and felt something warm and soft next to him. His eyes shot open. A slow smile crossed his lips. Consuela lay curled up against him, her face that of a young and innocent woman, but the night they had spent together put any idea of her innocence to the lie. She had made love like an experienced woman.

Slocum idly wondered again if Don Ynocente knew of her skills. Was this why his old friend was so eager to see Consuela returned? Somehow, Slocum didn't think so. The way Ynocente had spoken of Consuela Suarez hadn't carried any hint of her being the don's mistress. No lust had tinged the man's words, but something more than simple honor seemed to be involved. Slocum wished he knew what. If Consuela let it slip how they'd spent the night locked in each other's arms, even an old friendship with Ynocente Ochoa might evaporate.

Slocum didn't need any more enemies in Texas or across the border in Mexico.

Without disturbing Consuela, Slocum pulled his arm free and moved from under the blanket. The sharp, chilly bite of a desert morning cut at his body like a frozen razor. He shivered and gathered his clothes, slipping outside as he put them on.

The sun had come up over the Hueco Mountains. The cold lingering in the air belied what would happen later in the day. Slocum liked the piercing differences in temperature. The days were hot and the nights cold. That gave definition to his existence and a change from the sameness of the dusty cattle towns he rode through.

Slocum dashed icy water in his face and sputtered, coming entirely awake. When the last vestiges of sleep had left his ears he heard a disturbing sound. The click of a horse's hoof against stone echoed down from above. He hadn't checked the night before but he didn't think anyone had passed this way in several weeks, maybe months. He belted on his Colt Navy and eased off the thong from over the hammer.

He made his way downhill toward the ravine. He stopped and stared. Not ten yards away the sandy arroyo bottom had been kicked up by at least four horses. If he subtracted his and Consuela's horses, that meant a pair of riders had found them. Slocum's sharp green eyes worked over the scene until he saw where one rider had gone up the arroyo embankment.

He turned and looked over his shoulder. That would be the rider he had heard upslope. What had happened to the other? He drew his Colt and began looking. It took only a few minutes to find the second rider's trail.

He heaved a sigh of relief. As far as he could tell, there were only the two men. If he had to face more than this, he'd be in a world of trouble.

He dropped to his belly when he heard a cartridge lever into the chamber of a rifle. The distinctive *click* carried in the cold morning air, but he wouldn't have heard it if he hadn't been so close to the would-be killer.

Slocum slithered over a boulder like a lizard and poised on top, peering down. The man he spied on leaned his rifle against the rock and drew his revolver, checking the cylinder to be sure of smooth firing action. Slocum never hesitated. This was the best chance he was likely to get.

He spun about and slid down the rounded boulder, the friction tearing at his denims as he went. He landed with both boots on the man's shoulders. The unexpected weight carried the man forward onto his face. His six-shooter went spinning and he ended up a couple of yards from his rifle.

The man spat gravel and sand from his mouth and tried to shout for help. Slocum used his pistol like a club. The solid blow on the top of the man's head cut off any hope of warning his partner. Slocum stepped away, ready to use the Colt if the man hadn't been knocked out.

Slocum shook his head when he saw that the man was unconscious. Using his pistol like this was going to ruin the front sights. He used the tip of his finger to wipe off blood and bits of scalp left from its latest use as a bludgeon.

Slocum grunted as he rolled the man over. He sat down heavily and stared when he saw the deputy marshal's badge pinned on the man's leather vest. No matter what he did, he got in deeper with the law.

Slocum took the man's Colt and the Winchester resting against the boulder and made his way back toward the shack. With any luck, he could get rid of the other deputy before Consuela awoke. She need never know there had been any problem.

As he stalked the second lawman, Slocum wondered where the deputies had picked up his trail. He had been clever, even if he hadn't had time to disguise his trail properly. The only conclusion that made sense was Consuela. People noticed the rich, beautiful *señorita* and remembered her. Short of putting her into sackcloth and shoving a burlap bag over her head, Slocum didn't see any way of avoiding this unwanted attention. Men saw her and wanted her. Women saw her and hated her for her wealth and beauty.

But all remembered Consuela Suarez.

The slope got steeper. Slocum holstered his Colt and shoved the captured six-shooter into his belt so that he could use both hands on the Winchester. He found it difficult to get up the rocky grade without making noise. He strained to hear the man somewhere above him.

Only the faint whine of wind down the canyon disturbed the cold morning stillness.

Slocum circled a hill and came out behind it. A horse had been tethered to a mesquite tree. He advanced slowly, making sure he wasn't walking into a trap. He smiled grimly when he saw the man's back. The deputy thought he had Slocum in the trap.

Slocum cautiously advanced but the horse's sudden neighing brought the deputy around. For a split second fear registered on Luke Manning's face when he recognized Slocum—and that his prey wasn't where he had thought.

Slocum brought up the Winchester in a smooth motion and fired. Manning gasped as the bullet crashed into his leg. Reflex action caused him to squeeze the trigger of his own carbine. The bullet went wild, singing off rocks as it headed up into the mountains.

"Damn you!" Luke Manning screamed. "You can't take my woman. You're gonna die, you son of a bitch!"

Slocum chambered another round and squeezed off his shot. It took Manning in the other leg. The deputy wasn't going anywhere, not wounded in both legs.

Then Slocum had to duck for cover. Manning had recovered his wits enough to lower the muzzle of his rifle and try to center on Slocum's chest. The bullet still rose too high, but it cut a notch in the brim of Slocum's Stetson.

"You won't get away with this," Manning called, his voice weak. "My brother Frank's gonna eat your ears for breakfast. And Marshal Campbell will carve you up."

Slocum slid to his right, circling and going for higher ground. He got to the top of a big boulder and sighted down at Manning. The deputy had chosen his spot for the bushwhacking well. The shack's only entrance was an easy shot from here and if Slocum had kicked out the back, the other deputy would have been in good position for a killing shot.

The tables had turned, but Slocum did not squeeze the trigger. He stared down at Manning. The deputy was propped against a rock, his rifle slightly askew. Slocum kicked a rock down the side of the boulder to get Manning's attention. The deputy did not move.

Slocum cautiously slid down the rock and advanced on the deputy. His sightless eyes were already glazing with white film. His pasty face showed Slocum the cause of death. One bullet had cut the deputy's femoral artery. It had taken him less than two minutes to bleed to death. The sandy soil had sucked up the man's lifeblood and left only a dark brown trace on the surface.

"You stupid bastard," Slocum said, shaking his head. Slocum threw down the Winchester and went downslope to the shack where Consuela was just coming out.

"What was that?" she asked. "I thought I heard shots." Her dark eyes fastened on the extra pistol shoved into Slocum's gunbelt.

"Just doing some practicing. Doesn't pay to get rusty." He pulled the captured six-shooter out and tossed it into the shack. "To pay for the accommodations," he said.

"But—"

Slocum cut her off. "Let's ride. The sooner we're across the Rio Grande, the better I'll like it."

Consuela nodded, staring at him curiously. She said nothing, though, and for that Slocum was glad. He wasn't sure how the woman would take it if he told her he had just killed her lover.

They rode hard and crossed into Mexico two hours before sunset.

"Pedro will see to his daughter," Ynocente Ochoa said, watching as his foreman helped a weary Consuela into the hacienda. Ochoa turned to Slocum and extended his hand. "Again, I am in your debt, John. Simple thanks cannot ever be enough for what you have done."

"Then offer me a bath and a hot meal and good bed to

sleep in tonight, Don Ynocente." Slocum ached all over. The hard ride had taken as much out of him as it had out of Consuela.

"First, a drink. Come, you need it, *amigo*."

Slocum wasn't about to argue. There had been little time to eat, much less ease the desert-sized thirst he'd worked up. Even the fiery tequila tasted good going down. For a moment it was cool, then it turned into liquid flames in his belly.

"There was some trouble you ought to know about, Ynocente," Slocum said, after considering how best to tell his friend what had happened.

"With her young lover? The deputy?" Ynocente's voice sounded brittle and as sharp-edged as broken glass.

"Luke Manning."

The don's eyebrows shot up and his swarthy face turned darker as a storm cloud of anger crossed over it. "I will kill the son of a bitch."

"No need." Slocum downed another shot of tequila. He felt his tired, tense muscles beginning to relax.

"You have taken care of this, too?"

"He and another deputy tracked us out of El Paso. We'd've been back yesterday if we hadn't run into them," Slocum lied. He hoped that Ynocente did not question him too closely about what had happened before Manning had found them at the miner's shack. He wouldn't like lying to his friend, but Slocum knew he might have to if he wanted to leave the hacienda alive.

"His brothers will not be pleased with this."

"I doubt they will," allowed Slocum, "but they can't know for certain who's responsible. I left the other deputy alive; he never saw my face. Luke had recognized me as the one who pistol-whipped George Campbell, but he's dead now. I may be able to ride back into El Paso and not find myself in a world of woe."

"That is good. I did not mean for my feud with the Manning brothers to become yours, too, *amigo*."

Slocum and Ynocente sat and drank in the peaceful solitude of the hacienda courtyard until half the bottle had been drained. Only then did Ynocente say, "I cannot offer you enough money as reward for returning Consuela."

"That's all right, because I won't take anything. We owe each other too much, Ynocente. We go back many years."

"*Sí*, the cattle rustling days. They seem so long ago."

"They were."

"But rustling is still much on my mind these days. I do not rustle, no, my good friend, not I. There is no need. But I am plagued by rustlers."

Slocum waited. Don Ynocente was building to something.

"I have reason to believe a friend of the Mannings, a Johnny Hale, has stolen cows of great value from me and my brother."

Slocum looked across the tiled courtyard at the small pond. A fish surfaced and dined from an incautious insect. A small breeze stirred the potted plants and caused a fragrant, moíst, earthy odor to rise. Slocum reflected on what a perfect setting this was to get a man to agree to something he didn't want to do.

"What would it take to get your stolen cattle back?" he asked.

"There is not money enough to give you for returning Consuela to me. For the cattle, I will give you ten dollars a head."

"That's mighty generous. It must also mean getting them back is mighty dangerous."

"This Hale is not likely to admit to such thievery. The Mannings control the other side of the border, just as Don Juan and I control this side. The difference is that we no longer depend on stolen beeves for our income. They do."

Slocum saw that complaining to the El Paso marshal wouldn't get Don Ynocente anywhere. Captain Baylor of the Texas Rangers might not be much better. And no rancher could allow rustlers to operate unchecked. To do so only encouraged more thefts.

"With a few vaqueros to help you, it might be possible to find these cows that have 'wandered' across the Rio Grande and 'got lost' on Hale's ranch. Our brands are most distinctive and difficult to run."

Slocum knew that a good brand runner could take any brand and change it into something that looked totally different. Even the famous XIT had been run into a Star Cross brand by a clever rustler.

"How long have these wandering cattle been gone?" he asked.

"Less than a week. Pedro reported their theft to me only this morning."

"And you're sure they're on Hale's ranch?"

"Of course I am, John. There is a pattern, a rhythm, to the way things are done along the border. The cows can be no other place. Hale has them."

"I'll go see what I can turn up," Slocum said. The promise of ten dollars a head was generous. If he returned only a dozen, he'd have enough stake to get over into New Mexico Territory or even into Tucson in style. More than that, he felt he still owed Ynocente Ochoa for much. Returning Consuela had gone a long way toward erasing that debt. This would finish it off.

Slocum downed the last of the tequila and headed for a bath and a troubled sleep. He kept reaching for the lovely Consuela in the night.

6

John Slocum turned in the saddle, straining to catch a glimpse of Consuela Suarez. The woman was nowhere in sight. Only her father Pedro and Don Ynocente had risen to bid Slocum farewell.

"These vaqueros with you," said Pedro, "are very, very good men. They will not let your back go unguarded."

Slocum looked at the three men with him. They had the look of range riders about them, not gunfighters. If they found the cattle with the Ochoa brand, these three would work long and well getting the herd back across the Rio Grande. In any fight, though, Slocum had little confidence in them.

"I wish I could spare Pedro to go with you," said Ynocente Ochoa, "but there is much trouble to the south. My brother is sending many men to deal with this crisis among our peons. Pedro is the best I can send to tend to this disagreeable chore." Ynocente looked up at Slocum and said softly, "and you, *amigo,* are the best I can send to find our beeves on Hale's ranch."

"I hope it'll be easy," said Slocum. He didn't think it would be. Johnny Hale hadn't looked stupid when Slocum had seen him in the El Paso saloon talking with Frank and Doc Manning. There was no reason for him to keep the cattle in plain sight until the brands could be changed.

Finding the cattle would be hard—and if Hale had guards posted, the chore would be that much harder.

"Vaya con Díos," Don Ynocente said.

Slocum nodded and rode out slowly, still trying to catch sight of Consuela. He wondered if Ynocente or Pedro Suarez had told her that he was going back across the border this morning. Probably not. Ynocente Ochoa was no one's fool. He had to know that his foreman's daughter was beautiful and that Slocum had been on the trail for a long time. Slocum smiled as he remembered the many times he, Ynocente, and Juan had lingered in the whorehouses along the Texas–Mexico border so many years ago.

Slocum pushed those memories away. He had work to do. He settled in for the ride, becoming one with the motion of the powerful stallion under him. Slocum didn't quite sleep as they headed north to El Paso, but he came close. When they reached the *chamizal,* one vaquero motioned toward New Mexico Territory.

"There. In that direction lies Hale's ranch," the man said.

"I forded the Rio Grande yesterday," said Slocum, "not three miles from here. Is there a better place?"

The vaquero motioned to show there was. The river had begun to quiet. The spring runoffs were taking a rest, possibly to return with a treacherous surge or unpredictably to dry up to little more than a trickle. Slocum followed the other's lead, glad to avoid crossing near the outskirts of El Paso. The deputy he had left in the mountains might know his name but he couldn't know what he looked like—not for sure. Luke Manning might have described him, but it had to end there. Even Marshal Campbell couldn't remember his face. For such a small favor, Slocum thanked Lady Luck.

On the Texas side of the river, they made their way north, picking their trail carefully. Slocum kept an eye peeled for signs that a small herd had been driven by recently, but he saw nothing. Incessant desert wind erased any spoor likely to have been left by the cattle.

When they had got almost to Newman, New Mexico, he reined in and stared at a signpost by the road. The Circle H brand had been burned into a wood plank and nailed to a fence post. No other identification was needed, he decided. This was the Hale spread, and anyone riding along here would know it.

"*Señor* Slocum," the vaquero who spoke the best English said, "we believe that the pen with the cattle stolen from Don Ynocente is in that direction."

Slocum scowled at this information. Ynocente Ochoa hadn't been entirely truthful with him. He already knew where the cattle were. The vaquero's words were an admission of this. Ynocente had hired Slocum's gun, not his tracking abilities.

Still, Slocum had promised to do what he could, just as he had to return Consuela. If he were clever enough, Johnny Hale might never know the cattle had been stolen back. And getting paid ten dollars a head was mighty attractive to him.

"How long would it take you to get the cattle back across the Rio Grande?" he asked.

"Twice as long as it took to arrive. Perhaps four hours, *señor.*"

Slocum wondered if he could create enough of a diversion to keep Hale and his hired hands busy that long. He scowled. He would have to. There was no other way they could ride out with the cattle and not be stopped dead.

Slocum glanced in the direction of Hale's ranch house, then gestured for the vaqueros to follow him. He crossed the ground at a steady clip until he came to the pens where half a dozen head of cattle milled about.

"So few!" exclaimed the vaquero beside him. "More than fifty were taken. To recover so few will disappoint Don Ynocente."

"We wouldn't want to do that, would we?" Slocum said.

He dismounted and went to the pen. The cattle inside clearly carried the Ochoa brand. None had a brand looking like the Circle H he had seen on the sign, though he saw how the Ochoa brand could be changed with some work. Slocum walked around the pen and found the embers of a branding fire. In the ashes rested a branding iron.

The curious pattern would fit neatly over the Ochoa brand and run it into a lopsided Circle H. In disgust, Slocum threw the branding iron back into the ashes. He had nothing much against cattle rustlers. He and Ynocente Ochoa had done enough of it in their own day not to pay much mind to such thieving, but Slocum liked to see it done well. This branding iron was crude.

When he had rustled cattle, the brands he'd run were undetectable from the real ones.

"Just no pride of workmanship any more," he grumbled.

"*Señor* Slocum," said the vaquero. "We have big trouble."

Slocum spun and saw Johnny Hale and three men riding up from off the range. The vaqueros already reached for their six-shooters. Slocum ordered them to put away their pistols.

"Let's talk a bit first. *Then* we can shoot it out. We're sitting plumb in the middle of a den of rattlesnakes. I don't have a hankering to get bit by them."

"What you doing here?" Johnny Hale yelled.

"Just checking on Don Juan Ochoa's cattle. Probably one or two of Don Ynocente's in the pen, too." Slocum saw the way Hale's eyes darted toward the cold fire where the running iron rested. Hale didn't know how much Slocum had seen—or suspected.

Slocum wanted to keep it that way. To shoot it out, even with both sides numerically equal, was foolish. Hale could summon a dozen more cowboys whenever he wanted.

"Who are you? You ain't one of the don's men. You ain't no Mexican," Hale said suspiciously, his hand resting on the butt of his six-shooter.

"An old friend of the family. Don Ynocente asked me to ride along with his boys here and check on his cattle. It's right neighborly of you to take care of them like this. Fool cows shouldn't wander off like they did."

Slocum had given Hale a chance to back down. If he did and let them have these few head of cattle, they could ride out. If Hale wouldn't turn tail, there'd be blood spilled. Plenty of it, too, if Slocum was any judge of such things.

"We had three men bushwhacked a month back," Hale said, his hand still on his six-shooter. "Thompson, O'Neal, and Cain were found with bullets in their backs. Don't reckon you'd know anything about that, would you?"

Slocum felt rather than saw two vaqueros shifting position. From the tension in the air, he thought that they might know something about the murder of Hale's hired hands. Slocum let out a breath he hadn't even known he was holding. Don Ynocente had dumped him blind and stupid in the middle of a range war. Slocum would have to get out of it the best way he could.

"Can't say that I do," Slocum said. "Been all manner of bad things happening around here. The shooting of your men, the rustling of these cattle."

"You're accusing me of stealing these scrawny beeves?" roared Johnny Hale.

Slocum saw the man's hand tense on the butt of his pistol. This was all the warning he had to get his own Colt Navy out and into action. The hammer came back and fell on a cartridge; the pistol bucked in his hand and sent Johnny Hale spinning around. Hale's six-shooter had come free from his holster, but he fired too soon and the slug dug a trench in the ground at Slocum's feet.

All hell broke loose. The three vaqueros had unlimbered their rifles from their saddle sheaths and were firing at the cowboys. They showed more enthusiasm for the noise their rifles made than for marksmanship, Slocum noticed. The cowhands took no chances with so much lead flying through the air. They dived for cover, their pistols out and waving about.

"*Señor* Slocum, we have them on the run!" cried one vaquero. "Death to the gringos!"

Slocum crouched behind a fence post and felt buck naked. The slender salt cedar post gave damned little protection for him, and Hale's men had recovered from their initial surprise. He had hoped they would retreat, but they'd been in enough fights to know they would end up with a slug in the spine if they did. They stayed and fought.

Slocum glanced around and saw a chance for getting to real cover. Two bales of hay had been dropped a dozen paces away. He fired quickly three times as he made a run for the bales. One slug ripped the hat from his head. Another sent a lance of fire up his leg. He tumbled head first, got his bearings, and rolled behind the protecting hay.

"You all right?" one of the vaqueros called.

"I'm fine." Slocum poked his head above the bale of hay and drew fire. He emptied his pistol, then ducked back to reload.

"Kill the bastards, men!" Hale bellowed.

A cow let out a mournful lowing, then sagged against the pen. The posts gave way under the dead weight.

"Don't kill the damned beeves, you fools," Hale snapped. Slocum took the opportunity to look around one bale edge and fire at Hale. This drove the rustler to cover a dozen yards back in a stand of scrub oak just now putting out their few scraggly light green leaves.

The vaquero who spoke the best English dived behind the hay bale and joined Slocum. "What do we do now?" he asked. "They have the position on us. We are trapped in the open."

Slocum had already seen this. Hale's men had pulled back and had found good cover. Even with the vaqueros' superior firepower, the situation didn't look too bright to Slocum. They were pinned down, away from their horses that had shied at the first gunshots, away from decent cover, and on Hale's home ground. The gunfire would attract other cowboys the way shit draws flies.

Slocum became very aware of how far it was to the border and the safety of Don Ynocente's side of the Rio Grande.

"Circle back in that direction. Get the cattle between us and them."

"But they will shot Don Ynocente's cows!" The vaquero seemed genuinely stunned at the idea.

"Better the damn cattle than us. Move!"

Slocum gave him no time to think. Rising and firing, Slocum ran for the dubious safety offered by the cattle pen. Hot lead whistled past his head. He scooped up his hat as he ran, getting a new bullet hole in the crown from a near miss. Slocum thanked his lucky stars that he had not been wearing the hat when the bullet went through.

He tripped and fell face forward into the dirt just as a fusillade of bullets tore through the air where he had been. He rolled and fired wildly, trying to make Hale's men duck for cover. He failed. They became bolder, and one got winged by a providential rifle bullet.

"He hit me, Johnny!" the man moaned. Slocum knew that the cowboy wasn't badly wounded. When this penetrated his thick skull, he'd get mad and there'd be no stopping him—or Hale.

"Let us have the cattle and we're gone!" Slocum shouted.

"Get 'em!" came Hale's reply.

Two more of the cattle were killed in the deadly rain of lead. Slocum wiggled into the pen and sidled up to one carcass. It would stop any bullet Hale could fire at him, but it changed nothing. Slocum had to get out of the death trap.

It looked even bleaker to him now than it had before. His and the vaqueros' horses had run off during the shootout. He was running low on ammunition and reloading the percussion-cap Colt Navy took a spell to do right.

Slocum about surrendered when he heard the heavy pounding of horses' hooves. He knew that more of Hale's men had come to rescue their boss.

"How many rounds you have left?" he asked the vaquero crouching next to him.

"Twenty rounds. Less," came the disappointing answer.

Slocum saw that the other two were little better off. The thundering horses drew nearer. They had to make their bid for freedom now or they would die next to the slaughtered cattle, their blood mixing with that flowing from the cows' scrawny carcasses.

"We make a run for the barn," Slocum told them. "Don't worry about being accurate. Just keep them dodging. Ready?" He saw the frightened expressions on their faces. He hoped his own looked more confident.

"Now!"

The four men rose and began firing wildly and ran hell-bent for leather toward the distant barn. Halfway there, Slocum ran out of ammunition. He didn't want to think about why the others had stopped firing. He put his head down and sprinted, waiting for the bullet from Johnny Hale's pistol that would shatter his spine.

7

John Slocum swerved to the left, then ducked and threw himself to the right in an attempt to avoid Johnny Hale's bullets.

He landed in the dirt, panting and safe, just inside the barn's battered, unpainted main door. Slocum couldn't believe his good luck. He was still alive.

For a few seconds, he wondered what was wrong. He checked himself. His Colt was empty and he had a slight wound that seeped slowly, but other than these minor problems, he couldn't figure out what bothered him.

Then it came to him. No shots sounded outside.

He peered out cautiously and saw that the riders had arrived. Four men, still in the saddle, separated him from the three vaqueros. Slocum took the time to reload his pistol. The few extra seconds didn't matter. Whoever the riders were, they had stopped the gunfight. Hale stood out in the open, his six-shooter dangling from his index finger by the trigger guard.

After he had reloaded, Slocum slipped out of the barn, still wary. The newcomers might not have come to rescue him as much as to stop Hale. A few more corpses on the ground might not matter to them.

When he saw the glint of sunlight off the circular badges, Slocum went cold inside.

Texas Rangers!

"Hey, you, back there by the barn. Get your ass out here. Right now! And don't even think of using that gun of yours!" There was no denying the snap of command in that voice.

"Who are you?" Slocum called.

"Captain Baylor, Texas Rangers, you goddamn idiot. Put that gun away and get over here."

Slocum did as he was told. He didn't think his description as a Ranger killer had circulated, but he dared not take the chance. To run would only attract unwanted attention. If he kept his mouth shut, he might walk away from this.

"What started this, Hale?" Captain Baylor demanded. Slocum noticed that the Ranger didn't dismount and kept his hand on the butt of his ancient Colt Patterson. "You don't usually backshoot men on your own property."

"Don't go sayin' things like that, Baylor," snapped Hale. "You got no call accusing me of anything. These Mexicans came waltzin' in like they owned the place and tried to take cattle from my pen."

Captain Baylor glanced from Hale to the dead cattle in the pen. Two more had been shot down. Only six milled about, wanting out to find safety in some serene pasture.

"Those don't look like your brands, Johnny," the Ranger said in a low voice that made Hale shift nervously from foot to foot. Slocum saw the man's knuckles turn whiter on the butt of his pistol, but he made no move to lift it and shoot the Ranger captain. From the way the other three Texas Rangers watched him like hawks, Slocum and Hale knew that would be suicidal.

"We been watching the range real close, Baylor, ever since three of my men were backshot."

"Cain, O'Neal, and Thompson," a curly-haired, freckled Ranger told Captain Baylor. The officer motioned his man to silence, as if he already knew all this.

"We've been looking around to see who might have gunned those three down," said Captain Baylor, "but there's no witnesses or proof."

"It was some of Ochoa's men. He ain't got the balls to do it himself, but these gunslingers we caught trying to steal our beeves. They might be the ones!"

Slocum moved forward. He suspected two of the three with him of having done the crime. He had to divert attention, or the wily Captain Baylor would read the guilt on the vaqueros' faces.

"The brands on the cattle aren't Hale's," Slocum spoke up.

"What's your interest in this?" Baylor asked, hardly giving Slocum a second look.

"Not much. Don Ynocente hired me to ride along with his hired hands. His men don't speak English too well and he didn't want them getting into trouble."

"Fat lot of good you've been, then," said Captain Baylor.

"I guess I got confused. We saw the cattle with the Ochoa brand and thought these gents had penned them up for us. We didn't know they were trying to *steal* the cows."

Baylor laughed at this perversion of the truth. Slocum tried to remember everything he had heard about the Ranger captain. There wasn't much good. Captain Baylor's sense of the law depended a great deal on how much money was offered. He had been busted in rank three or four times for taking bribes, but he had always managed to work his way back up to high rank. Slocum had even heard rumors that Captain Baylor wasn't above using the law to get rid of men, if the price was high enough. It wouldn't surprise Slocum to find out that the Manning brothers had Baylor in their hip pocket. They controlled El Paso, and Baylor went where the money was.

"These beeves don't look like you were too careful in branding, Johnny," said the Ranger officer.

"Not ours," Hale admitted. He scowled, as if daring Slocum to challenge him again. "It's like he said. We just penned them up, waiting for someone to come and get them."

"Don't reckon you ever thought of letting Don Juan hear about your good deed."

Hale scowled even more ferociously. "We just rounded them up. Haven't had time to do squat about the scrawny cows. Take them and good riddance!"

"There are more," spoke up the vaquero to Slocum's right. "Fifty head or more were—" He grunted when Slocum elbowed him in the ribs.

"Don Juan lost fifty head. Don Ynocente sent us to look for them. Do you think the other cattle might be running loose on your ranch?"

"No." Hale's denial was sharp and emphatic.

"Why don't you gents just take the beeves still standing and get them across the border to Don Juan or Don Ynocente or whoever sent you," suggested Captain Baylor. The captain cocked his head to one side. "You got enough men around to handle this? Can't see that Ochoa would send just the four of you to fetch his beeves." Baylor glanced around as if he expected the entire Mexican army to pop up from hiding. Slocum did nothing to change this mistaken notion on the Ranger captain's part. Let the lawman think a thousand soldiers would ride down on him if any more shooting happened.

"Wait a minute," Hale snapped. "How do we know they were sent by Ochoa? *They* might be rustlers."

"Don't be dumber than you have to be, Johnny," said Baylor. "Rustlers don't dress like that, and their horses have the Ochoa brand on their rumps. The Mexicans aren't rustlers, but the gringo has the look of one." For the first time, Captain Baylor stared at Slocum.

Cold, dark eyes stripped Slocum to the soul, but Slocum didn't flinch. Baylor's lip curled in a slight sneer. The two men understood each other too well.

"See that the Mexicans get the cattle across the border before sundown. I'd hate to have to come looking for y'all and give you a hand." The threat was obvious. Captain

Baylor wanted Ochoa's men out of Texas or he'd shoot them down like mad dogs.

Slocum spoke quickly to the vaquero and told him to get the cattle out of the pen and moving back toward the Rio Grande. They could worry about crossing the river after they had left the Hale ranch. The three vaqueros found their horses and mounted. Once they were in the saddle, it became apparent that they were expert at their jobs. The few remaining cattle tried to separate once they were outside the pen. The vaqueros kept them in a tight knot, moving toward the distant road.

Slocum climbed onto his stallion and looked at the Texas Ranger captain. Baylor's face showed only contempt. No hint of recognition flickered in those flinty, dark eyes. The Ranger knew a killer was on the loose, but he did not suspect Slocum of having committed the crime.

With the conditions along the border as touchy as they were, Slocum doubted if a killing down Van Horn way mattered much here. If it did, Captain Baylor would only look to see how he could profit from it.

"What brought you out here?" Slocum asked.

"Just passing by," said Baylor. "Now ride, damn your eyes! I don't have any call explaining shit to you, mister." The Texas Ranger captain glared at Slocum, who touched the brim of his battered Stetson and reined his stallion around. Slocum gained nothing by riling up the Ranger. He galloped out and caught up with the vaqueros. The tiny herd required only one of them to keep it moving.

"*Señor* Slocum, those men with Hale," said the vaquero with the best English. "We know they stole Don Ynocente's beeves. Why does not the Ranger captain arrest them?"

"We're lucky to get away from there in one piece, *amigo*," said Slocum.

"But there are more Ochoa branded cattle on this ranch. There *must* be."

"I agree, but there's nothing we're going to gain by

calling them on it. I suspect Captain Baylor might be mixed up in the rustling, though I doubt it. There'd be no reason to let us go."

"Don Juan is *el jéfe político* in Paso del Norte and is very powerful. He is becoming angry at the losses from our herds," said the vaquero.

"That might be part of it." Slocum wondered how frightened of a small army backing them up the Ranger captain had been. It seemed to have weighed heavy on his mind—enough to let them go with the surviving cattle. "Something tells me Captain Baylor has bigger fish to fry than a few paltry cows. If letting us go back into Mexico with these cattle soothes ruffled feathers, he might figure that's a small price to pay."

"Don Ynocente wanted us to return with *all* the stolen beeves," the vaquero insisted.

"Let's make do with these," said Slocum. "We can think through what it'll take to find the others." Even as he spoke, he went cold inside. Something had turned very, very wrong.

He spun in the saddle. He and the vaquero were alone with the tiny herd. The two vaqueros he suspected of bushwhacking Hale's three men had vanished.

"Where are they?" Slocum demanded.

"Jorge and Tomás?" asked the vaquero. "They might be riding to find their *nóvias*, their lovers."

"Bullshit. They went to find the rest of the cattle," said Slocum. He sagged. He should have know that Ynocente Ochoa had planned than he had revealed to Slocum. Slocum had handled the gunplay on the Hale ranch as he had been expected to. The vaqueros had been ordered to bring back all the cattle—and maybe they had been told not to return to the hacienda until the job was done. Whatever had happened, Slocum was no longer in charge.

"Perhaps they seek the cattle," the vaquero said, shrugging expressively. "Who can say?"

"Those three men of Hale's who were murdered—what part did Tomás and Jorge have in that?"

The vaquero's face tightened into a swarthy mask. "Cain shot down women and children to steal the beeves. The other two had the bad luck of being with him when Tomás found him."

"Can you get the cattle to the river by yourself?"

"These few? But of course, *señor*. What are you going to do?"

"Find Jorge and Tomás before they cut down any more cowhands and *really* get Hale mad."

Slocum wheeled around and backtracked until he found the place where the two vaqueros had left. He tried to reconstruct in his mind how they had left without him noticing. He had been lost in thought. All they had to do was stop and let Slocum ride on, and he hadn't noticed. Slocum knew it accomplished nothing, kicking himself for letting the vaqueros sneak off and return to the Hale spread. He didn't have eyes in the back of his head. Don Ynocente hadn't hired him to look after these men.

He stewed as he rode, telling himself over and over that nothing would happen, that Tomás and Jorge wouldn't find any cattle, that there wouldn't be any trouble. Slocum doubted it all. They *would* find the cattle, and there would be hell to pay.

Jorge and Tomás faced not only Hale's men but the four Texas Rangers. Slocum had never known a Ranger to be well disposed toward a Mexican—and especially not after Captain Baylor's warning about getting across the border before sundown.

Slocum followed the two vaqueros' trail easily. The dried sod had broken under their horses' hooves, making the trail distinct. The wind would erode the trail in an hour or less. Should a rare spring rain drench the area, Slocum would lose the trail almost instantly. He looked into the clear blue sky and smiled. There would be no rain today or any time soon. It was a typical desert spring day.

He came to the top of a small rise and looked down into a grassy bowl dotted with burgeoning trees and scattered blue and yellow flowered plants. He caught sight of the vaqueros. Slocum waved his hat, hoping to attract their attention. Either they did not see him or they ignored him. He couldn't tell which.

Slocum sat and watched as the two men rode across the grassland, their heads down. Slocum guessed that they were on the trail of the cattle. He stood in his stirrups and scanned the countryside. Small clouds of dust rose from beyond the far side of the depression. On a slight breeze blowing hotly over the land rode the lowing of cattle. Jorge and Tomás had found cattle, but did they carry Ochoa branding on their hips? Only close inspection would tell.

Slocum settled down in the saddle and let out a long sigh. It might take him twenty minutes' hard riding to catch up with the vaqueros. By then they would have examined the herd.

Slocum just hoped that they avoided starting a range war.

He started down the rim of the grassy bowl. Halfway to the bottom he saw a new cloud of dust moving to his left. He paused, squinting to get a clearer view. The first cloud came from a herd of cattle. It hovered and didn't move much, except when the wind caught up the edges and whipped them over the landscape. This cloud moved with a speed equal to a trotting horse.

Or many trotting horses.

Slocum put the spurs to his stallion. The animal neighed and looked back at him with an accusing eye. Slocum patted the horse's neck and soothed him. "Get us there, old boy," Slocum said. "I'll see that you get the finest oats for this."

The horse snorted skeptically but obeyed. Like the very wind they flew across the grasslands. Slocum reined in before they came to the upslope. He had no intention of driving his horse so hard that the beast dropped from exhaustion. He got off and walked the horse to the rise.

Slocum went cold inside when he saw what went on below.

Jorge and Tomás had dismounted and wandered through the large herd, examining brands. From their gestures he knew that they had found most of the rustled Ochoa cattle.

The riders he had seen, two of Johnny Hale's men, came up a ravine, hidden from the vaqueros. When the men burst up and over the rim of the arroyo, they had their pistols out.

Slocum drew his Colt Navy and fired a shot into the air. At this range he couldn't hope to hit anything, but the sound alerted Tomás and Jorge. They saw the bushwhackers riding down hard on them.

Slocum was too far away to hear what was said, but he clearly saw the vaqueros raise their hands over their heads in surrender.

He also clearly saw the two cowboys sight and fire. One Mexican slumped to the ground. The other saw the mistake in trying to surrender. He fumbled for the pistol holstered at his hip. Half a dozen rounds ripped through him as both of Hale's men opened fire.

Slocum's anger burned like a forest fire and tore at his guts. There wasn't a damned thing he could do about this slaughter. He watched one cowboy go over and urge his horse to kick at the fallen vaqueros. Then he lifted his pistol and began firing rapidly into the air. The cattle finally got it through their dim brains that they should run from this annoyance.

They stampeded, trampling the fallen bodies. Slocum tugged at his horse's reins. There was nothing he could do now against Hale's men. Jorge and Tomás were dead. But Slocum would return to settle the score.

8

Slocum stopped and stared down the long, muddy slope leading to the ford across the Rio Grande. The lone vaquero had already driven the tiny herd to the Mexican side. On the far bank Ynocente Ochoa walked through the small herd of starved cows, examining each one and shaking his head sadly at their condition. More trouble came for the don. Slocum knew how his old friend would take the news of the other men's deaths.

The entire border might explode in a blood feud. Slocum shifted his weight slightly in the saddle, trying to find a comfortable position. It wasn't possible. His rear end would be the least of his worries soon enough. Too much ill will had been built up over the past few months for anything less than range war to occur. It didn't matter that Jorge and Tomás had bushwhacked three of Hale's men. All that would count to Don Ynocente was the loss of his own two men.

Slocum had to admit that for once Ynocente Ochoa seemed to have good cause for shedding gringo blood. He didn't doubt that the two vaqueros had found the Ochoa brand on the other cattle. Johnny Hale had rustled the cattle, and Jorge and Tomás had been within their rights to get them back, even if it meant backshooting.

Cattle rustlers got hanged with some regularity in this part of Texas. Tomás and Jorge had just brought three to justice with their pistols rather than a knotted rope. Now they lay dead, trampled by the very cattle they had sought to retrieve.

Slocum turned even grimmer. When Luke Manning's death became widely known, the Manning brothers would ignite the powder keg that was El Paso, even if Ynocente Ochoa didn't. It wouldn't take much for Doc and Frank Manning to learn that their hot-headed younger brother had been romancing the beautiful daughter of Ynocente Ochoa's foreman. Hell, they might know already.

Slocum dismounted and walked his stallion to the slippery riverbank. He waved to Ynocente, who waved back. No matter how he cut it, he had to deliver the bad news to the Mexican *patrón*.

"Slocum, behind you. On the bank!" Ynocente shouted.

Slocum looked over his shoulder. The range war had started sooner than he had anticipated. Johnny Hale and a full dozen of his cowboys stood outlined against the blue sky, sunlight reflecting off their blued rifle barrels. Slocum couldn't run; they would cut him down. Trying to fight didn't look promising, either.

Slocum dragged out his Winchester and prepared to die.

He levered a round into the chamber when an ear-splitting roar came from across the river. Slocum saw as many as ten vaqueros kneeling, working their carbines, preparing for another barrage. Like those who had ridden with him to the Circle H, they were more enthusiastic than good in their marksmanship.

"Hurry, Slocum!" came Ynocente's voice. "Cross the Rio Grande! We will lay down covering fire for you!"

Slocum jerked when the first of Hale's bullets came after him, barely missing the top of his head. Slocum jerked on his horse's reins and got the black stallion into a small stand of creosote bushes growing on a sandbar. He knelt, using a branch of the tree for a gun rest. He squeezed off a shot. His days as a sniper in the Confederate Army came back to him in a rush. His shot found its target.

One less cowboy to stop him.

But the remaining men had a mind to keep him pinned down. Bullets ripped through the branches around him. One grazed the tree limb where he rested his rifle and sent sap and splinters into his face, momentarily blinding him.

If it hadn't been for the charge Ynocente led across the river, Slocum knew that Hale would have gunned him down. Ochoa shouted and waved his huge sombrero—and he had vaqueros backing him up, with their rifles firing wildly. What they lacked in accuracy they made up for in courage.

Hale hesitated, and this gave Slocum the time to get the wood and sap away from his eyes. He swung his rifle around and fired quickly, wounding two cowboys who were trying to ride him down. They bent low over their horses' necks and raced hell-bent for leather for the cover afforded by the ridge and Hale's other gunmen.

"John, are you all right?" Ynocente demanded, dropping from his horse and slipping in the wet sand. "You are not hurt?"

"I'm all right."

"You have been hurt."

"That happened earlier," Slocum said, dismissing the wound he had received in the gunfight back at Hale's barn. "We've got to get across the river. We don't dare stay here. They'll get Marshal Campbell involved and all hell will be out for lunch."

"Pah!" spat Ynocente. "I care nothing for that *pata cojo*. He cannot stand against my valiant men!"

"Probably not," muttered Slocum, thinking that the drunken marshal had trouble standing without someone helping him. But the marshal had resources that could be tapped eventually. A telegram to Washington, money for a posse, more deputies, even cavalry loaned from Fort Bliss would turn the tide against Ynocente. George Campbell didn't have to be good. He just had to be loud enough to bring down the entire U. S. side on the *patrón*.

Slocum saw the way Ynocente's men formed a ragged line. Against men dug in on higher ground, this was suicidal, but he wasn't going to have them charge. All they needed to do was get back across the river. Hale wouldn't follow. The tables would be turned. Ynocente's brother, as chief political officer of Paso del Norte, could call on the resources of an entire nation. From all he had seen of the Mexican Army in the past, Slocum knew they weren't very good at soldiering, but there were one hell of a lot of them.

"Where are the others?" asked Ynocente.

"What others?"

"Tomás and Jorge." Ynocente Ochoa stopped and stared open-mouthed at Slocum as realization dawned on him.

"Two of Hale's men gunned them down. They'd found the rest of your cattle when they snuck up on them. They tried to surrender. The two gunned them down while their hands were in the air."

"The swine!" Ynocente turned red in the face and began rattling off a string of Spanish curses so complicated that Slocum couldn't follow them. "I will have their balls for this! I will cut them off and use them for target practice."

"Ynocente—"

"No!" the *patrón* cried. "I will *not* cut their balls off. I will leave them in place, *then* use them for target practice. And I am not a good marksman."

"Ynocente," Slocum finally cut in. "Your men are dead. We will be, too, if we don't get out of here."

Ynocente Ochoa ignored him and stormed off, oblivious to the hot lead flying through the air around him. He spoke quickly to Pedro Suarez. Slocum saw Suarez turn pale, then bob his head up and down as if he were a marionette and Ynocente yanked his strings. The ranch foreman rushed to his horse and got on the animal, ignoring its attempts to shy away as bullets sang through the air around them.

Like some insane cavalry commander, Pedro Suarez

pulled out his pistol and aimed it uphill. Slocum heard Suarez issue the command to attack.

"Ynocente, don't make him do it." Slocum saw his warning came far too late. The vaqueros had mounted and formed a wedge. They put the spurs to their horses and charged Hale's position.

Johnny Hale had scant opportunity to dig in. If he had the time to fortify he would have massacred Suarez and the others. Still, his position on the high ground was good and his men saw that they dared not turn tail and run. Most stood and fired into the rank of attacking Mexican vaqueros.

"You fool," Slocum shouted, shaking Ynocente. The man seemed oblivious to all that happened. Slocum shook his friend again. Ynocente came out of his coma, a dark cloud drifting over his face.

"I will kill them all for what they have done this day. They cannot steal my beeves, murder my loyal men, kidnap my . . . my foreman's daughter."

"That's not what happened with Consuela," said Slocum, "and you damned well know it. Luke Manning didn't kidnap her. She went willingly with him."

"Lies!" screamed Ynocente.

"Manning's dead. I killed him myself," Slocum said, trying a different approach. "And a hell of a lot of your men will die here, too, unless you stop them." He stared at the rough line and the huge gaps cut in it by Hale's fusillade. Fully half of Ynocente's vaqueros had fallen. Those on the ground stirred and moaned in pain. Slocum didn't think any had been killed but all had been seriously wounded. The rest continued in the futile assault.

"They show their true colors. The cowards! They break and run before my charge!"

"They're regrouping, not retreating. I passed a stand of mesquite. They'll pull back to that and cut your men down like a knife going through fresh butter when they attack again."

"No, we will drive those sons of bitches back to Hale's ranch. We will drive them all from the territory!"

Bloodlust totally possessed Ynocente Ochoa and kept him from thinking rationally. He began struggling up the hill. Blood from his fallen men mixed with the dirt and turned the hill even more slippery.

Slocum saw what the *patrón* did not. Clouds of dust rose in the direction of El Paso. The gunfire had attracted attention. Come from the center of the town, that could only mean reinforcements came to help Hale. The marshal would have told Frank or Doc Manning, and they would have dispatched a small army.

Slocum reloaded his rifle and swung into the saddle. He couldn't save Ynocente by himself, but he might give the man time to come to his senses and save himself. There was no safety in numbers. Not any longer the charging vaqueros had been reduced to only three. Miraculously, Pedro Suarez still clung to his saddle horn, wobbling about and severely wounded—but he lived.

Slocum knew that Ynocente was beyond reason. Suarez might be able to get the battered remnants of the vaquero force turned back toward the border. None like to retreat. If they didn't, though, Slocum saw no way for any to survive.

His horse struggled up the slippery slope. From there the going got easier—and harder. Slocum tried to stop himself from watching the slow progress of Marshal Campbell and the men with him as they rode ever closer. When they arrived, the battle would be over. Permanently.

"Pedro!" Slocum called out. He rode alongside the foreman and grabbed to keep Pedro from falling out of the saddle. A half dozen spots oozed blood onto his shirt. He had been hit too many times to keep going much longer.

"*Señor* Slocum, thank you for what you did for my Consuela." Pedro's eyes rolled up. Slocum refused to let the man die in peace. He shook him hard.

Pedro's eyes came open slowly. His face was pulled

back into a grimace from the pain. "Let me die in peace. I beg you."

"You've got to get the vaqueros turned around. Order them back to Mexico."

"Don Ynocente wanted us to avenge the deaths of Tomás and Jorge."

"By dying yourself?" Slocum shook Suarez again. The horses moved about under them and Hale's barrage had hardly slackened, though Slocum knew the man must be running out of ammunition. Hale hadn't prepared for a siege any more than Ynocente Ochoa had.

"If that is Don Ynocente's wish."

"Think of Consuela," Slocum said desperately. The marshal and half a dozen fresh men rode hard to join the battle. "You'll never see her again. You don't want her to be an orphan, do you?" Slocum had never heard anyone mention the girl's mother, Pedro would have, he knew. That meant Consuela's mother must be dead.

"Don Ynocente, he will look after her. He is a good man."

"And these are good men dying uselessly. Get them back across the Rio Grande and we can mount a *real* attack on Hale and the Mannings. This half-assed fight is getting us slaughtered like cattle!"

Suarez coughed and spat blood. "You will lead us? With your knowledge, you will do this thing?"

"Yes, dammit, yes!" Slocum was ready to promise anything. Marshal Campbell almost fell out of his saddle in his attempt to stop his horse and get to the ground beside Johnny Hale. Even at this distance Slocum saw that the lawman was dead drunk.

Better dead drunk than dead, Slocum thought.

"*¡Retírete!*" called Suarez in a surprisingly strong voice. The handful of vaqueros remaining in their saddles immediately broke off their futile attack. None had wanted to continue this suicidal charge into Hale's rifles.

"Thank you," Slocum said. He was almost pulled from

the saddle by Suarez's weight. The man had slumped forward, unable to remain erect. He stirred weakly, letting Slocum know he still lived but could not ride. Slocum heaved and pulled Suarez over the saddle in front of him. The dead weight cut of the circulation in his legs, but Slocum knew this was only temporary. Either he got away from Hale and Campbell or he died on the spot, as so many others had done.

Bending over, he urged the stallion to its utmost. The horse strove valiantly to get back up the slope and down the muddy enbankment. This time Slocum did not pause when he got to the Rio Grande. He urged the horse straight across. The vaqueros who had fallen had already come this way. There had to be a bottom to the river he couldn't see in the muddy, turbulent flow.

There was. The stallion slipped twice on its way across and then gained its footing on the Mexican side of the river.

Slocum clumsily lowered Pedro Suarez to the ground and turned back. Ynocente Ochoa remained on the U. S. side of the river. Slocum reined in and waited when he saw Ynocente helping two wounded men across.

Ynocente dropped one to the ground beside Suarez. The other stumbled off on his own.

"I could not let them stay and be captured. Those pigs will execute any who lived through this."

"Never charge when the enemy holds the high ground. Even if you outnumber them," said Slocum. On the far side of the Rio Grande Marshal Campbell and Johnny Hale stood and shouted insults. "Do you think they will come after us?"

"Into my country? Do not be stupid, my good friend. My brother runs Paso del Norte with an iron fist. Those," Ynocente said, spitting in the direction of Texas, "dare not enter."

Slocum said nothing. This had escalated beyond his worst nightmare. Ochoa's vaqueros had bushwhacked three of Hale's men, after Hale had rustled the cattle on this side of the river. Now more men lay dead. Jorge and Tomás. Possibly some of those injured who had made it back into Mexico. Slocum saw two men with severe injuries nearby. Slocum did a quick count. Ynocente had not lost any men outright, but all were wounded to some degree. Of Hale's men, Slocum hadn't a clue. He had wounded two or three. Possibly six others had fallen. Although Slocum could not be sure, he thought Campbell had lost at least one of the men with him.

Too many had reason to rue this day.

"They will pay for this," Ynocente Ochoa said grimly. "Those gringos will pay dearly. I must speak with my brother. Juan knows how to deal with their kind." Ynocente swung up into the saddle and rode off without a backward glance.

From across the Rio Grande Hale shouted. "This means war, dammit. You can't come invading into the United States of America like that. We'll stomp your asses into the mud!"

Slocum helped the wounded onto their horses to start the long ride back to the Ochoa hacienda. Don Ynocente had not invaded the United States. That all-out attack had been a reflex action on his part, and, as much as it bothered Slocum admit it, Ynocente had come to his rescue. If the don had not attacked when he had, Hale would have blown Slocum into bloody tatters.

What bothered Slocum the most was knowing that more would die before tempers quieted on both sides.

9

Slocum dropped to the ground and then eased Pedro Suarez off the horse. With a heave, Slocum got the heavy foreman over his shoulder and carried him into the hacienda. The coolness and serenity of the inner courtyard did nothing to soothe the rage Slocum felt. Ynocente Ochoa had been stupid. He should never have tried to rush Johnny Hale without being prepared for it. Now there was hell to pay all along the border, and too many men had been needlessly wounded.

He lowered Suarez into a chair. The man had somehow survived six bullets in the chest and the long ride back from the river. His eyes fluttered open and he tried to speak. Only choking noises came from his lips.

"Take it easy," Slocum told him. "We'll see to your wounds." Slocum pulled out a thick-bladed knife from a sheath at the back of his belt and used the sharp tip to slice away what he could of Suarez's shirt. Blood had caked the cotton cloth to the man's flesh.

Suarez moaned softly and closed his eyes again. Slocum thought the foreman might have fainted. If so, that was for the best. He got as much of the shirt off Suarez as he could, then began working to soak off the rest. The blood parted only after several minutes of gentle work and toweling with a piece of cloth dipped in water from a fountain.

Slocum studied the wounds and shook his head. Some

men were born lucky, and Pedro Suarez was one of them. Six gunshot wounds, two serious, the rest little more than bloody scratches. And of the two that had bit deep, neither seemed to have punctured a lung. The bloody froth Suarez had spit up had come from biting his tongue.

"Who? Oh, it's you, John," came a familiar voice. Slocum looked up to see Consuela Suarez coming from the section of the house where the unmarried women were quartered. "I hadn't expected you back today. *Madre de Díos* but you are all bloody!"

"Not mine," Slocum said. Consuela walked around and for the first time saw her father. One hand flew to her mouth and she turned pale.

"Don't faint," Slocum said irritably. "I need help—*he* needs help."

"What can I do?"

"Bring hot water and disinfectant, if you have it. If not, bring me a bottle of tequila with a worm in it."

"What?" the woman asked, startled out of her shock at seeing her father so badly wounded. "*¿Con gusano?*"

"The worm sucks up the poisons in the tequila. I want alcohol as pure as you can get it."

Consuela nodded and hurried off. In a few minutes she returned with the tequila and several of the servants. One woman tried to push Slocum away, but he was too intent on getting the bullet out of Suarez's chest. The bullet had smashed into a rib and followed the bone around, but had not penetrated further. Slocum poured a generous measure of tequila onto the wound as he worked his knife point under the bullet. With a quick, smooth flick, he got the lead slug out. That left the second one buried between ribs.

"How may I help you?" Consuela asked. Her voice trembled slightly, but she showed no other sign now of being affected by the blood oozing from her father's wounds.

"Get him patched up. There, there. Use clean bandages after you've washed the wounds thoroughly."

"We have done this before."

Slocum looked into the woman's dark eyes. They were wide and round and a trace of fear lurked there, but he also saw courage. She was frightened for her father's safety, but she wasn't going to shriek and run away. Not until the worst was over, and maybe not even then.

Slocum used the edge of the knife to slice open a deep channel in Suarez's side that bled like a son of bitch. Through the blood he found the other bullet lodged in a muscle. Slocum tried not to do too much damage, but the bleeding made his hands slippery, and he knew it was better to remove the bullet than to worry about scars and a little blood. Blood poisoning always led to death.

"Please, *Señor* Slocum," said the woman Slocum thought was Consuela's *dueña*. "I am expert at the sewing. I will take care of closing the wound."

"Reckon you might be better at that. He's lost a lot of blood. Be careful with him. And get some men to carry him to his quarters. Pedro's going to have to rest up a spell before he's fit again."

"He will be all right?" asked Consuela. "You are not just saying this?"

"No," answered Slocum, looking directly into her dark eyes. "He's a lucky man."

"You were there. That made him very lucky," she said, averting her eyes.

Slocum said nothing. Just being on the banks of the Rio Grande today meant sour luck. Slocum couldn't blame Ynocente too much for what had happened, but someone had to take the blame. If Ochoa hadn't ordered his men to charge Hale's position, damned near two dozen men might still be unscathed. Slocum had been in skirmishes during the War where fewer had been shot up.

"What is wrong, John?" Consuela asked.

"Nothing."

"Is this something Don Ynocente had done? He has been like a crazy man for weeks. All he talks of is how the

Manning brothers are destroying what he has worked for. Don Juan is even worse. The pair talk of expeditions of troops to invade Texas, to take on the El Paso marshal and the Texas Rangers. And for what? A few miserable beeves."

"The cattle are important," Slocum said, "but not to the point of starting a border war. There are better ways of stopping Hale and the Mannings."

"You will not abandon Don Ynocente, will you? He trusts you. There are so few who share his confidences these days."

"Ynocente and Juan and I go back a long way," Slocum said, remembering some of their earlier exploits. They had been wild in those days. He shook his head. "But I won't lead any army into Texas. They'd be the worst thing possible."

"What is the best?"

To that, he didn't have a good answer.

"This Hale, he has taken our cattle."

"Two vaqueros bushwhacked three of Hale's men," Slocum said.

"There has been more than one raid onto our land. Women have been raped and severely beaten. These men of Hale's, did they take part in this raid?" she asked.

Slocum shrugged. There was no way to tell what had started the blood feud. Little things, something big, nothing at all. Who knew? It had gone too far to figure out how it had begun.

"You don't seem overly concerned," he said. "You took off with Luke Manning."

"He was very persuasive. He made me think that we could stop this before it grew."

"You're one lying bitch," Slocum said. "But you're still the most beautiful woman I have ever seen."

Consuela smiled, and it wasn't an innocent grin. "Luke excited me. The danger of being with him filled me with lust." She put her fingers lightly on the front of Slocum's soiled, blood-streaked shirt and drew her fingers up and down, the nails digging into his chest. "He excited me, but not half as much as you do."

"You're still a lying bitch."

"Let me show you the truth of what I say." The finger-nails dug deeper and she curled her fingers like a cougar with its prey. She pulled him closer. A quick kiss set his pulse racing. "I owe you much for saving my father. Let me repay you."

Slocum looked around. Consuela's maid had accompanied the men taking Pedro to his bed. They were alone in the courtyard. Slocum felt himself responding powerfully to Consuela. Ynocente might not be back for sometime. He wasn't sure where the don had gone; possibly Ynocente went to consult with his brother Juan. That might mean he'd be gone for a day or more. Still, Slocum hesitated.

Consuela didn't. Her fingers slipped under his shirt and worked against naked flesh. Then she bent forward, her sharp teeth working on his buttons. She bit them off, one at a time.

"Don't," he protested, but his heart wasn't in it. He knew this was crazy. If anyone saw them, he would be lucky to escape with his life. Ynocente protected the women of his hacienda—all the women. Slocum still wasn't sure that Consuela didn't rate special attention from the don. She obviously meant more to him that the mere daughter of a valued worker and foreman.

Consuela spat. Two buttons ricocheted off a green and white tiled wall. She grinned broadly and buried her face once more in his chest. He put his arms around her. There was no stopping her—and he didn't want her to stop. Slocum cursed himself for his stupidity in giving in to carnal pleasure, but Consuela Suarez fired lust in his loins.

She finished pulling the buttons off, then drew her soft lips up his belly and chest, gently kissing here and there, leaving wet spots wherever her flicking tongue touched.

Slocum stroked her glossy black hair and simply enjoyed the sensations flooding through him. He had been beaten up and shot and he ached all over. Consuela's eager mouth changed all that. He came fully alive, his body responding until his denim jeans felt down right painful.

Before he could say a word about it, Consuela found this problem. The way she solved it suited Slocum just fine. Her fingers slipped past the brass buttons and popped open his fly. Slocum moaned softly when his hard length snapped free of the prison of his trousers.

"What have we here?" Consuela said in mock surprise. "Why, can it be a snake about to bite me?"

"Never," Slocum assured her.

"Is it a stick? It is hard like one." She batted his trobbing manhood around with the tips of her fingers. More blood pumped into the lust-engorged length and Slocum thought he would die.

"Don't," he cautioned. "I feel like a stick of dynamite with its fuse lit."

"A fire? There's a fire?" Consuela fumbled around inside his jeans and drew out his balls. She stroked over them with her fingers, then knelt, looking up at him. "A fire should be put out. Where will we ever find enough water? I must smother this fire that has taken hold within you."

Her ruby lips circled him. Slocum groaned and almost lost his balance. He moved carefully, not wanting to dislodge her from this worshipful post at his groin. Her lips moved slowly up and down his length while her fingers massaged his hairy pouch.

Slocum propped himself against a chair, his legs too weak to hold him upright any longer. His fingers worked through her shining dark hair, guiding her head in a slow, smooth rhythm that excited him even more. His hips began heaving. No matter how he tried to stop himself, he couldn't do it.

"Do not worry," she said, her mouth momentarily empty. "I know how to handle such things."

"I noticed." Words failed him when she again en-mouthed his hardness. Her hands circled his body and gripped his ass. She tightened her grip and pulled him closer. He thought he would spear her all the way down her throat, but Consuela moved her head at the last possible instant. She sucked hard on him as her lips slid off the purple tip of his cock.

He jerked free of her mouth. Only iron control kept him from shooting off. Like a snake, Consuela wiggled up his body. Somehow as she moved she managed to open the front of her bright blouse and exposed her firm, ripe breasts.

"My turn," Slocum said, burying his face between them. He worked his way up one brown slope and got to the hard nipple. He sucked as hard as Consuela had on him. She moaned and shoved her chest forward, silently demanding more. He gave it to her.

She bent back and opened her frilly embroidered blouse fully. What he saw within excited him even more. Slocum gasped when her nimble fingers again found his steely length and began tugging.

"I can't hold on much longer with you doing that."

"Then don't!" She lifted a slender leg and hooked it around his waist. He fumbled and got her skirt raised. To his delight he found she wasn't wearing anything under it. She pulled him directly to the spot where they both wanted him to go. His throbbing manhood touched moistness, parted her puckered nether lips, and then plunged into tight hotness.

Slocum swayed as he supported her entire weight. Consuela threw her arms around his neck and lifted her other foot off the floor. Both legs locked securely around Slocum's waist. She clung to him, her mouth seeking his.

He bounced slightly, causing her to lift and fall on his buried length. The slight action thrilled both to the point where their desires took over from any rational control.

Slocum spun about, as if dancing with Consuela. The

woman's body rose and fell slightly, but each minute movement felt like an earthquake to them. She tensed and relaxed hidden muscles and gave Slocum an even more thrilling time than she had with her mouth.

He kissed and bit at her lips, his arms around her waist. Her breasts crushed passionately against his strong chest. His breath came faster and he spun around and around. Consuela leaned back, her long black hair streaming outward.

"Yes, John, yes, *sí!*" She closed her eyes and her face went slack with the intensity of her emotions. "Do not stop. Keep moving. I need it so!"

She hunched up and down even as he tried to sway his hips. The circular movement, her strong legs about his waist, the feel of her all around him caused the man's body to erupt. He shoved his hips outward hard even as Consuela gripped down powerfully on him.

Their passions peaked, then began to fade.

"You are leaving me," she said sadly after a few minutes. "Why do you do this to me?"

"You were too good," Slocum said. He pulled her upright. She unlocked her legs from his waist and stood close, the turgid nipples of her breasts still rubbing seductively against him.

"Am I good enough for you to do this again?" Her breath gusted hotly through the hair on his chest.

Slocum looked around. He wasn't sure when they would be discovered in the courtyard, but it wouldn't be much longer. They had been lucky—or else Consuela's *dueña* had seen them and looked the other way. He couldn't believe this for an instant. Don Ynocente was strict; the older woman would be even stricter when it came to upholding the morals of her young ward.

"We do not have to stay here," Consuela said in a husky voice. "You have a private room. Mine is so . . . public."

Slocum understood what she meant. An unmarried woman had little privacy in a Mexican household.

"We can always...bathe," Consuela said. "You are filthy and I know how to scrub a man's back."

Slocum remembered the luxurious bathhouse Ynocente had built behind his hacienda. It offered both privacy and the chance to clean off some of the grime caking his body.

Consuela saw the answer in his face. "*¡Bueno!*" she cried. "I will meet you there in one minute No more. One minute!"

Slocum watched the girl rush off. He experienced a pang of guilt about what they had done. He violated all the rules of honor with Consuela. He wasn't supposed to make love to a woman under Ynocente's care.

Somehow, Slocum didn't care. He remembered Consuela's passion and nothing else. Sharing it again mattered more than Ynocente's anger. Slocum went to his room and got fresh clothing, then hurried to the bathhouse.

Consuela waited for him, naked and willing in a large tub of water. He joined her in the hot, steamy bath and forgot all about the blood feud raging along the border.

10

Slocum finished toweling off and dressed slowly, paying more attention to the still-naked Consuela than to how he put on his clothes. When his Colt Navy slid from his holster and landed on the floor, he pulled himself away from the beautiful woman. She drew him powerfully; his Colt kept him from death.

He sat on a low bench and began stripping the pistol, checking it and making sure he had a full load in each cylinder. He usually carried the hammer on an empty cylinder to prevent an accidental firing, but he decided the extra round meant more than safety now. Conditions were too unsettled for anything but extreme caution.

"John?" Consuela rose from the soapy water and stroked over her arms and body, wiping off suds and water. He couldn't keep his eyes off her feminine perfection. "Is this to be over soon?"

"What? Between us?"

"No, not that. Will Don Ynocente and Don Juan be able to resolve their fight with the Mannings?"

Slocum shook his head. He had no good answers for questions like this. "Neither side is willing to give an inch," he said. "Trying to look at it from both sides doesn't tell me who's to blame."

"*They* are!" flared Consuela.

"From this side of the river, that's how it looks. Johnny

89

Hale's men saw nothing wrong with murdering Tomás and Jorge because they had gunned down three of his cowboys."

"They stole our beeves!"

"And before that?" He watched her expression.

"There was the—" She cut off her words abruptly. "How do you know of these things?"

"Just a guess, nothing more. There's no telling how this feud started. I reckon it's been festering for a long time. When you've got powerful men on each side of the border, it's inevitable that there'll be fighting sooner or later."

"You take the Mannings' part in this."

"Hardly. I'm saying that Ynocente might not have done all he could to avoid fighting." He couldn't get the suicide charge up the muddy banks of the Rio Grande out of his mind. He had seen worse. Pickett's Charge ranked up there with the most blockheaded military action taken by any general, but Ynocente had nothing to gain and everything to lose when he had so senselessly attacked Hale. Honor meant nothing if you were all alone and men who trusted you were dead on the ground.

Slocum chewed on the idea that Ynocente had tried to sacrifice his men intentionally. Slocum was in no position to complain. They had pulled his bacon out of the fire, but Ynocente might have had other reasons for his attack. If enough of his vaqueros died, it made his claims against the Mannings even stronger. Those deaths might even solidify the don's position among other *patrónes* reluctant to fight the Texas ranchers. Being powerful had never been enough for Ynocente, even when Slocum had ridden with him.

Ynocente Ochoa had to be top gun. Nothing less than complete control mattered to him. Did it rankle him that Frank Manning had a bigger ranch? Was he angered by Doc Manning's power in El Paso politics? Did even Ynocente's brother being Paso del Norte's *jéfe político* help soothe the longing for total power along the Rio Grande?

Slocum had no answers for these questions either, but

they made Ynocente's behavior more understandable. Being cock of the walk would appeal to Ynocente.

"Dry me," Consuela ordered. Slocum looked up and smiled wickedly. She had tired him out, but they could still have some fun. He picked up a towel and went to the woman. He flipped the towel around and caught the flying end, so that the towel circled through Consuela's legs. He moved the soft towel back and forth gently, stroking over the fleecy down between those firmly muscled legs. Consuela closed her dark eyes and leaned against him.

"That feels so good, but I wish something else was there."

"If I tried, I might just die of exhaustion," Slocum said. He had been through much today. His bouts of lovemaking with Consuela had left him feeling good, but he needed sleep more than anything else now. He used the towel to capture droplets of water running down her sleek nut-brown back and sides and took special care with her breasts.

Before he could finish the job properly, excited shouts sounded in the direction of the hacienda. Slocum dropped the towel and went to see what caused such a stir.

"Let them be, John," said Consuela in her sultry voice. "I need you more."

Slocum was drawn back but stopped, hand on his Colt. He had learned to tell the difference between shouts of anger and those of fear. Whoever had screamed had been terrified.

"I'll be back," he said.

"Do not expect me to wait for you."

Slocum barely heard. He was straining too hard to pick up other clues about the disturbance. In the distance he heard horses coming fast. He started to go to the stables to saddle his own horse, but turned instead for the hacienda. He heard frantic rushing around inside now. He ran down the short tunnel leading to the courtyard. Several women were fumbling with rifles, endangering themselves and those around more than Slocum liked.

"What's wrong?" he demanded.

For an answer he got a rapid burst of Spanish from the older woman who was Consuela's maid. Slocum was slow to decipher, but when he did he raced for the front entrance. He skidded to a halt just as the first of Johnny Hale's men reined in.

Slocum reacted a fraction of an instant faster than any of them. His hand flew to his Colt and he pulled it out. As he moved, he cocked the pistol and fired in one smooth motion. The bullet sang its deadly song before Hale's cowboy had the chance to lift the clumsy double-barreled shotgun he carried. Slocum's bullet caught him on the side of the head. The man jerked upright and tumbled from the saddle. His spooked horse reared and bolted. The rider had one foot caught in a stirrup and was dragged away.

Slocum ran forward and retrieved the damascus barrel shotgun, cocked both hammers, and set his feet wide. He hardly aimed as he triggered the first load. The shotgun bucked hard and the 00 buckshot took another rider from horseback. The second barrel accomplished nothing but keeping the rest of Hale's men at bay.

"You're the one what rode with them damned greasers," Hale called out, "I recognize you. You was down at the river, too."

"Don Ynocente saved me from getting shot up by you yahoos," Slocum said. He threw aside the empty shotgun. He felt vulnerable facing down a score of armed men with nothing more than five shots left in his Colt. Nothing in his stance betrayed that fear.

"We don't cotton none to getting our asses kicked," Hale called. "We came over to do a little ass-kicking ourselves."

"Ride on back across the river," Slocum advised. "You don't want to be buried on this side of the Rio Grande."

"What's your stake in this? You're a gringo. Why are you sidin' with those backshootin' greasers?"

"The Ochoas are my friends," Slocum said. He figured that the longer they shouted insults at each other, the better off he was. If Hale ever took it into his head to start shooting, it would be over in a flash—and Slocum knew who would come out on the short end.

"You pick lousy friends," Hale said. Slocum never saw the gesture that brought a rain of lead down on him. One of Hale's men might have taken it on himself to open fire, or Hale might have signaled. Slocum didn't much care. He was too busy dodging death.

Slocum got off three shots that didn't amount to a hill of beans, then found a fleshy human target with the fourth. One shot remaining, he dived and rolled, kicking up a cloud of dust. Obscured momentarily, he had the chance to come to his knees and take careful aim. His sights centered on Johnny Hale's body. He squeezed off the round just as Hale's horse bucked.

Slocum missed with his last shot, and Hale spotted Slocum in the middle of the settling dust cloud.

"There he is! Cut him down!"

Slocum winced as a bullet grazed his upper left arm. Another cut a shallow notch in his ear. Unable to take time to reload, Slocum turned tail and ran for the safety afforded by the hacienda's thick adobe walls. He dived and landed on his belly in the cool tunnel leading in to the courtyard. Above him whined bullet after bullet.

"Get down!" he shouted at the women gathered just inside the courtyard. "Stay back!"

One made a small noise and sank to the ground. Slocum wriggled forward on his stomach and got to her. A chance bullet had gone into her right temple—and hadn't come out on the other side. He shuddered at the idea of the bullet bouncing around inside the woman's skull. It had carried enough velocity to enter her head but not enough to break through on the far side. He pushed her back, marvelling at how peaceful she looked. Only a tiny drop of blood marked the bullet's entry point. She might have simply fainted.

But she hadn't fainted. She was dead.

Slocum picked up the fallen woman's ancient carbine and got a round into the chamber. He rolled over and, lying prone, began firing down the dark passageway. Only occasional riders sped by outside for him to take a shot at, but the slow fire kept up the pressure on Hale's men.

"What do we do, *Señor* Slocum?" asked one of the women.

"Pray," he said.

"We are doing that. What else is there?"

"Watch the other corridors into the courtyard. Hale might try to attack down them. And have someone watch the roof. He might come over the top to get to us."

Slocum feared a hundred things simultaneously. One saving grace was the hacienda's lack of outer windows. A solid adobe wall faced the attackers and protected those within, unless Hale started throwing torches onto the roof. Slocum glanced back and heaved a sigh of relief on this score. The red-tiled roof would resist all but the most stubborn of attempts to set fire to it.

More slugs slammed into the dried mud walls and ricocheted back into the courtyard. Behind him the fancy patterned tile broke with a loud snap. Slocum kept his head down and tried to think of anything he had missed. Something kept nagging at him until he stiffened and rolled to sit up.

"Consuela," he shouted. "Where the hell's Consuela?"

"*Señor*, we have not seen her."

"Check her room. Find out if she's there." Slocum heard a horse's hooves in the corridor. He spun around and saw a rider bent low and trying to enter. Slocum couldn't get a clean shot at the man so he cut the horse out from under him. The animal squealed in pain, sounding more like a pig than a mare. Slocum hated the waste but he wasn't about to allow any of Hale's men into the central courtyard. If he did, the battle would be over.

The rider struggled in the narrow passage to get free of his dead horse. Slocum put them both out of their misery. His first shot silenced the cursing rider. The second put a merciful end to the horse. All things equal, Slocum would have preferred to kill just the horseman and save the horse.

"She is nowhere to be found," came the report. It took Slocum a second to gather his wits and realize that the maid spoke of Consuela.

"Did you look everywhere? *¿En todo el mundo?*"

"Everywhere," the maid assured him. "Is she all right?"

"How the hell should I know?" snapped Slocum. He thrusted the rifle at the woman and pointed down the hallway. "Shoot anyone coming in. Anyone, anyone at all, coming in."

"*Sí*, yes, yes!"

Slocum reloaded his Colt Navy and ran for the back of the hacienda. A young girl hunkered down by the entryway, her hands shaking as she clutched a rifle. Slocum patted her on the shoulder, then indicated that he was leaving.

"I've got to find out what Hale is up to," he said. This was only partly true. He didn't give a tinker's damn what Hale did, as long as he left everyone in the hacienda alone. Barns could be rebuilt and cattle replaced. What worried Slocum the most was some devilment that involved the women and children.

He slipped down the cool tunnel, his back pressed against the rough adobe. He glanced around a corner and saw a dozen of Hale's men at work near the corrals getting the horses out.

Slocum cursed. He didn't want his stallion taken. That was a damned fine animal and had served him well. His anger cooled a mite when he realized that the horse wasn't as important as Consuela. If she had returned from the bathhouse someone would have seen her. That meant she was cut off from the hacienda.

Slocum hoped that she'd had a chance to run. The ranch spread out over thousands of acres. A woman like Consuela must have a special place to hide out.

Slocum reacted when he saw two cowboys coming out of the barn leading his black stallion. They hadn't bothered stealing the saddle. The horse was enough for them.

Slocum made sure the horse carried too high a price for the cowboys. His first shot got the cowboy on the left in the gut. He doubled over, moaning. The man on the right took a second to figure out where the gunshot had come from. Slocum got off two more rounds. One caught the horse thief high in the shoulder and spun him around. As the black stallion bolted, Slocum took off after it.

He got his arms around the horse's neck and let the animal's forward speed throw him back and around. He managed to get his leg over the horse's back by the time Hale's men spotted him. Slocum kept low on the horse and outpaced the cowboys.

Away from the hacienda and the curtains of lead falling around him, Slocum reined up and soothed the frightened horse.

"There, old boy. It's all right. You're going to be just fine." But rising in his mind came an unanswered question: What had happened to Consuela?

Slocum settled on the animal's back, wishing he had a saddle. It had been some time since he'd ridden bareback. He used his knee to swing the stallion around while he fumbled out the ammunition and reloaded his Colt. He returned to the hacienda at a walk, looking for some sign that Consuela had escaped the bathhouse before Hale arrived.

He found no trace of her. At the rear of the bathhouse, Slocum dismounted and peered inside. His guts turned to ice when he saw the woman's clothing still scattered across the floor.

A hail of bullets made him look around. Johnny Hale

motioned for his men to retreat. They had emptied the corrals of Don Ynocente's fine horses and had set fire to the barn. They had shot up the outer walls of the hacienda but hadn't done much other visible damage.

How many of those inside they had killed, Slocum didn't know. He forgot about that entirely when he saw a ñaked woman struggling with two men by the corral.

"Consuela!" he shouted. Slocum vaulted onto his horse and pulled the animal around. He put his heels to the stallion's flanks about the time one cowboy got Consuela's hands tied behind her. Both men hoisted the kicking woman over the rump of Hale's horse. It took them only seconds to lash her down.

Johnny Hale let out a war whoop and galloped off, Consuela shrieking like a banshee. Slocum bent low and urged his horse to even great speed. He could catch Hale. The rancher's horse was weighed down with a double load.

But Slocum never reached Hale. He heard a tiny *pop!* as someone fired a small-caliber pistol. The flash of pain in his head was the last thing he remembered as he tumbled into the dirt.

11

John Slocum lived in a dark world filled with pain. He fought against it. His struggles only brought him more suffering. When intense jolts of pain lanced into his head, he trashed about, trying to make it go away.

"Easy," he heard through the burning fog inside his head. Slocum swung at the sound. His punch didn't land.

Fighting to get one eye open, he peered up at Ynocente Ochoa. It took several seconds for him to recognize the man. "What do you want?" he managed to croak out.

"He is all right," the don said in a relieved tone. "Help him to sit up. The wound is small, but his brains have been addled by the shock from the bullet."

When Ynocente said this, everything came rushing back to Slocum. He let the men with Ynocente help him to sit up, back against a cool adobe wall, then he pushed them away.

"Your fine horse is safe, my friend," Ynocente said, smiling. "You need not have chased after Hale's *banditos* like that. A few horses mean nothing."

"Have you been inside the hacienda?" demanded Slocum.

Ochoa's face hardened. "Why? Was anyone injured?"

"At least one woman was killed."

"Those swine!" Ynocente's anger flared anew.

"Did you stop Hale?"

"What? No. They had ridden off before we arrived. These are Juan's vaqueros who accompanied me. He thought I might need help around the rancho until I could recruit more to replace those lost on the other side of the river."

"You didn't see Hale at all?" asked Slocum, panic rising within him. Seeing Ynocente's confused expression at this question turned Slocum's panic to hellfire. He burned inside, fuming at himself for allowing Hale to kidnap Consuela. She had been safe once before when she ran away to be with Luke Manning. Not this time. Now she was Hale's captive.

Slocum didn't want to think about what the rancher might do with the lovely, naked Consuela.

"What is wrong, John?"

"Hale's got Consuela." Slocum was surprised at the way his voice sounded. It came out level and emotionless, but it sounded as if he spoke into a bucket. Every word rang hollow. Even worse, they echoed inside his head until he wanted to scream.

"No, not Consuela. You lie! I'll cut your lying tongue from your head!" Ynocente Ochoa pulled his fist back to strike Slocum. Consuela's *dueña* reached out and stopped him.

"Don Ynocente, please. He speaks the truth! I saw them riding off. They took her from the bathhouse." Tears rolled down the woman's cheeks. "Consuela had no clothes when they caught her."

'The pigs!" Ynocente spun and stormed off.

"Wait, what are you going to do?" called out Slocum. He had seen enough bloodshed and didn't want more. Left to Ynocente and his brother, the entire border would turn into a battleground.

"You have a better way of getting her back unharmed?"

"You know that might not be possible," said Slocum, hating himself for what he said but knowing he had to shock Ynocente enough to make him pause to think. "She might be beyond your reach."

"What are you saying, Slocum? I will not believe that even that pig Hale has killed her."

"I'm saying an army might not be able to rescue her. We've got to go slow and see if stealth won't work better than brute force."

"I want him, Slocum. For what this Johnny Hale has done, he will die!"

"After we get Consuela back, *then* think about what you want to do. Go charging in like a mad bull and he'll kill her, sure as sunrise."

"That might be for the best," spoke up Consuela's *dueña*. "They will have dishonored her."

Slocum held his tongue. The way these people thought, he was as guilty as Hale for having made love to Consuela. Whether it was rape or willingness, nothing but Consuela's "honor" mattered.

"You will sneak in and rescue her? Is this what you are saying?" The contempt in Don Ynocente's voice didn't surprise Slocum.

"There might be other ways. Captain Baylor doesn't want a bloodbath along the border."

"The Texas Ranger captain will bring her back? Pah!"

"There's no love lost between him and Marshal Campbell," Slocum said. "I might be able to play one off against the other."

"Campbell is no longer marshal in El Paso," said Ynocente. "Juan told me they have a new law officer. He is a former Ranger named Dallas Stoudenmirer. He will do nothing against Manning or Baylor. He is one of them."

"Stoudenmirer?" Slocum frowned. The name was familiar to him but he couldn't remember why. His head felt as if a hive of wild bees had taken up residence and made his ears buzz with their damnable activity. He had been through too much and he needed to rest up. Slocum knew that wasn't likely to happen—not if he wanted to stop a terrible range war along the border.

Through the haze of dull pain and buzzing, he asked himself why he should bother. Let everyone in El Paso hate those across the border in Paso del Norte. Let Ynocente shoot up the Mannings. Let this Stoudenmirer try to control it. Let them all go to hell.

Slocum shook his head. The pain clearing away such fuzzy thoughts. He owed nothing to Ynocente now—or to anyone but himself. The memory of Consuela Suarez kept coming to haunt him. If he wanted to keep a whole skin, he should ride on out and never be seen on this side of the Rio Grande again. But he couldn't as long as Consuela was a captive. He had seen what Johnny Hale was like. The idea of gunning down that son of a bitch appealed to him more and more.

"Give me some time to feel out this the new marshal. He might want to put things right."

"You have one day. I can wait no longer. Even this might be too long," said Ynocente Ochoa, shaking his head. "Poor Consuela! I want to save her, not avenge her."

Slocum hoped that Ynocente didn't have to avenge her, either. He heaved himself to his feet and went to saddle his stallion. It would be a long ride back across the river and into El Paso.

The river had subsided from its spring peak. Slocum marvelled at how swiftly the water had vanished. The churning current was still swift enough to take a man off a horse if he wasn't paying attention, but it was nothing like the flood crest it had been.

Slocum rode slowly down El Paso's Mesa Street, alert for trouble. The town seemed quieter than before. He wondered if this was an illusion or if something had happened. Dismounting across the street from the Ben Dowell Saloon, Slocum paused to unhook the leather thong across the hammer of his Colt. He wanted to be ready for anything when he walked into that snake pit.

His hand flashed to his pistol but he did not draw. The commotion came from inside the saloon. Frank Manning came sailing out the swinging doors to land heavily in the street. Following him came a burly man with a shotgun in hand.

"You dumb bastard," the man called after Manning. "You may own this place, but you don't own this town. *I* do now."

"You ain't been given the deed to El Paso, Stoudenmirer," Manning said, brushing himself off as he got up from the ground.

"I never did cotton to you, Frank. And your brother Doc is even worse. Nothing would please me more'n to blow your balls off. Think I'll start now." Stoudenmirer lifted the shotgun and cocked the double hammers.

"Wait a minute, Dallas. I didn't mean nothing by what I said."

"Don't make no never mind now, Frank. I got it into my head to blow you away—and I will!"

The roar of the shotgun sent Slocum ducking. Frank Manning was running for his life, though. Following the retreating man came Dallas Stoudenmirer's mocking laughter. "Always knew he was a yellow-bellied son of a bitch."

Slocum smiled wryly. He was taking a shine to Stoudenmirer's style. The new marshal had bearded Manning in his own saloon and sent him running with his tail tucked between his legs. Stoudenmirer might even be interest in hearing what Manning's henchman Hale had been up to, and willing to do something about it.

"Marshal, can I have a word with you?" Slocum called out.

"Who might you be?" Stoudenmirer worked at the tip of a bushy mustache to get it waxed end fashionably pointed again. "You look familiar. You're not with that scoundrel, are you?" The marshal used the muzzle of his shotgun to point in the direction Manning had taken.

"It's about him and Johnny Hale that I want to talk to you."

"Let's get out of the sun. All this marshal work is making me powerful thirsty." Stoudenmirer went back into the saloon, not appearing to care if Slocum followed or not.

Slocum entered cautiously. Stoudenmirer paid no need to anyone else in the saloon. Jake saw Slocum and smiled weakly. Business wasn't too good and Slocum had a good idea why. Stoudenmirer kept the paying customers away.

Stoudenmirer knocked back two shots of whiskey before Slocum even got to the bar. Jake poured a tequila and dropped down a foamy mug of beer beside it without asking.

"You drink that shit?" Stoudenmirer spat. "Not fit for man nor beast. Hell, not even Manning drinks it."

"You handled Frank Manning real good," Slocum said, trying to get around to telling Stoudenmirer about Consuela's kidnapping. "That must mean you're not in the Manning's hip pocket like George Campbell was."

Stoudenmirer spat and hit the spittoon with practiced ease. "Campbell was a fool. The city aldermen got fed up with him. But you ain't here to talk politics. I've seen that expression on men before. Something's eatin' you. Spit it out."

Slocum studied Stoudenmirer closer. The man's sandy-colored mustache drooped again, this time damp with droplets of whiskey. His blue eyes were close-set and he had a cruel look about him. Strong, scarred hands curled around the shot glass. He made that liquor seem like the most important thing in the world.

"You know Don Juan Ochoa and his brother Ynocente?"

"Know *of* them. They're the big wheels on the other side of the river. You work for them?"

"They're mighty riled because of what Johnny Hale has been doing to them."

Stoudenmirer snorted. "That bloodbath down by the river? That what you're talking about? Seems Hale gave more than he got."

"That's part of it. Hale has raided across the Rio Grande and stolen horses and cattle."

"Always thought the scum-sucker was a rustler. Those brands on his beeves never looked right." Stoudenmirer worked on another shot. Jake kept pouring and the marshal kept drinking.

"You seem to know a good deal about what's happening around here, being newly arrived and all," said Slocum.

"Wife's lived here for a couple years. I spent time with the Texas Rangers down Abilene way before hearing about this job."

Jake started to say something but a cold look from the marshal silenced him. The barkeep shoved the half-full bottle across and let Stoudenmirer pour his own.

Slocum saw Jake looking past him outside into the street. He turned toward his right and caught a moving reflection in the mirror behind the bar. Men gathered outside for the kill no longer content to be like vultures and wait for the marshal to die. They were going to kill him *now*. Slocum had wondered how long it would take Manning to bring back enough gunmen to handle this brash marshal.

Stoudenmirer seemed oblivious to the gathering storm outside. He drank steadily and the level of amber liquor in the bottle dropped.

"They hired me to quiet down this town. Don't like peaceful folks getting caught in the middle of damned shootouts between Mexicans and cattle rustlers, no sir."

Jake slipped along the bar, reached the far end, and bolted for the back room. Slocum turned so that his left side was toward the swinging door leading into the street. His hand rested on the handle of his Colt. He'd have his pistol out and firing in an instant should Manning burst through the doors.

"What you getting so antsy over, mister?" asked Stoudenmirer. "They're not going anywhere. They're waiting to gun me down. Better men than them's tried and failed." He polished off the last of the whiskey. Since he had chased off Frank Manning, the marshal had drunk almost half a quart of fiery liquor—and he didn't show a bit of it in his speech or the steadiness of his hand.

"Don't like getting shot up for nothing."

"Then you should hightail it out with the barkeep. Must be a back way. But I'd watch myself if I was you."

"Why's that?"

"Manning might think I'll go sneaking out and have a backshooter or two waiting there. A dozen places in the stable where a sniper might hide. Yep, at least that." Stoudenmirer strained to reach over the bar for another bottle. Nothing came to hand. He let out a deep sigh and broke open the shotgun, ejecting one spent, burned cardboard shell. Fumbling in his left vest pocket, he pulled out a fresh one and thrust it into the chamber.

"That going to be enough firepower?" Slocum asked.

"If you're volunteering, you're welcome, but damned if I'm going to pay you or pin any tin badge on your chest. You got to take your chances, like every other citizen of El Paso." He tapped the heavy gold badge on his own chest. "See this? A gift from my good friend Johnson over in Fort Worth."

Stoudenmirer's attitude left something to be desired, Slocum thought. He wasn't too anxious to go outside with the marshal and get himself ventilated, yet he didn't want to see the man walk into an ambush. Stoudenmirer didn't appear to care one whit what happened.

"You need any more shells?"

"Two will do me. They didn't bring an army, after all." Stoudenmirer patted his coat pocket, then reached into the left side and pulled out a bellygun. The Colt '71-'72 had its seven-inch barrel sawed down to less than three. The leather-lined pocket and the lack of front sights and cartridge ejector on this pistol insured a quick draw.

"Not very accurate for street shooting," observed Slocum. That .44 pistol would blow hell out of anyone at close range, but Stoudenmirer was heading out into the open for a fight. Manning wasn't likely to get near enough for the bellygun to be effective.

"Don't intend for it to be. Got its partner right here." The marshal pulled back his coat on the right side to show another Colt in a cross-draw holster, this one with its barrel intact. Both guns were easily reached by his left hand.

"There are other ways besides going out there to face them," said Slocum.

"What? Don't go telling me you're a lily-livered scum-sucker, too. I had you pegged for something more." Stoudenmirer spat. This time he missed the brass spittoon. "Time to earn the picayune pay they're giving me."

He never looked at Slocum as he pushed through the doors. Immediate gunfire sounded. The roar of Stoudenmirer's shotgun told Slocum that the marshal had lived this long. The second blast did nothing to quiet the whine of lead outside.

Slocum considered, then went to the swinging doors and peered out. Marshal Stoudenmirer looked to be his best chance for getting lawful help in tracking Hale and getting Consuela back. It wouldn't do to let Manning shoot the man down before he'd been on the job a week.

Slocum stared in amazement. Stoudenmirer had thrown away his empty shotgun and was using his long-barreled Colt. He stood in the center of the street, carefully aiming and squeezing off his shots, oblivious to everyone shooting at him.

Slocum drew his pistol, ready to join in. As quickly as the gunfight had started, it ended. Stoudenmirer spun, fired once, and brought down a man from the doorway across the street. The marshal twisted to one side, aimed high, and gutshot another man on the roof of the saloon. He came crashing to the ground, almost at Slocum's feet.

The sudden silence that descended on the town was more frightening than the gunshots. Stoudenmirer knocked out the spent brass from his Colt and reloaded. He strode back toward Slocum.

"You just going to stand there, or are you going to buy the marshal a drink?" Stoudenmirer pushed past him on his way back into the saloon. "Yes, sir, this marshal work surely does work up a man's thirst."

Slocum stared at the pair of men dead in the street, then followed Stoudenmirer inside. He had found the man best able to help him get Consuela back from Johnny Hale.

12

John Slocum sat across the table from Marshal Stoudenmirer and watched the man go through a full quart of cheap whiskey. After this much of the potent liquor, he wobbled slightly and his speech became a heavy Southern drawl. But if Slocum hadn't seem Stoudenmirer drinking so much, he would have thought he was almost sober.

"Nothing like a bunch of damnfool gunslingers to make a man thirsty. Isn't that right, Slocum?" Dallas Stoudenmirer fixed an icy blue stare on Slocum that belied the amount of liquor sloshing in his belly.

"You don't care much for the Manning brothers, do you?" Slocum countered. "Hale is one of their men. He might own his own ranch, but Frank says frog and Johnny Hale jumps."

"That's about the way I see it, more or less. What's it to you? You got the look of a drifter about you. Don't see roots going down anywhere around here." Stoudenmirer made a production out of studying Slocum's boots, as if examining them for taproots going down into the saloon floor. "Nope, you're like the damned tumbleweeds. First wind that comes along sends you bouncing along to God knows here."

Slocum saw something of a drunk's rambling in Stoudenmirer's words, yet he couldn't be sure exactly how sober the marshal really was. He had downed a quart and a half of liquor, and this was just what Slocum had seen. Evidence showed that he had been in the saloon for a spell before Slocum got back into El Paso.

"Hale might be a good way of getting back at Frank Manning."

"Who the hell cares about revenge? He ain't done nothing to me except rile me up a mite. I've been pissed off worse in my day." Stoudenmirer craned his head to one side. "I've seen you somewhere before. You ride up from the south?"

Slocum remembered what had been said about Dallas Stoudenmirer. A former Texas Ranger, and from Abilene. He might have heard about a Ranger killer. Not many men had the steel in them that Slocum did. The marshal might be fishing or he might know something and just be toying with him. Slocum was hard-pressed to decide which.

"Been here a while," he said. "Long enough to know there's a border war brewing if you don't do something about it."

"That hoo-haw down on the river don't count. The Mexicans asked for it. Should never have crossed the Rio Grande. The border's there to keep 'em on their own side." Stoudenmirer wiped the rim of his glass with his stubby forefinger and licked off the last of the whiskey. "Fact is, no one on this side's broke no laws for me to go throwing my weight around over."

"Hale raided Don Ynocente's ranch."

"You told me that. Stole some horses. That's Mexican law. Can't take time out from real work to go enforcing *their* laws."

Slocum said, "Hale kidnapped the daughter of Ochoa's foreman and brought her across the river. Her name is Consuela Suarez. Do you want Don Juan agreeing with his brother about bringing over Mexican troops to rescue her?"

"We got troops enough at Fort Bliss to take care of that. It's beyond my province, so to speak. Laws that get broken on *this* side of the river matter." Stoudenmirer signaled for more whiskey, then leaned back, balancing precariously on the two rear chair legs. "Don't get me wrong. I'd like to see Hale in jail, just to prove who's the boss in El Paso. Can't let the Manning boys get away with shit or they'll walk all over me."

"Like they did George Campbell."

"That bag of wind?" Stoudenmirer spat. "He wasn't owned by anybody. He *gave* himself away. Too dumb to even *sell* himself dear."

"I've heard tell that Captain Baylor would never make that mistake."

Slocum watched the marshal's reaction. The fury growing on Stoudenmirer's face at the mention of the Texas Ranger captain surprised him.

"Him? Don't mention *him* to me. He'd sell his soul to the Devil and then try to resell it to the Lord God Almighty."

Slocum wasn't sure if Stoudenmirer considered this a virtue or merely disliked Captain Baylor.

"Look at the trouble brewing. The Mannings are at the center of it. El Paso—and over in Paso del Norte—will be quiet if you stop them."

"I can do it."

Slocum shook his head. To this Stoudenmirer said, "Why don't you just get on that fine black horse of yours and ride on out of El Paso? There's no room for people agitating in these here parts. I don't reckon I'd like to see your face again, drifter."

"Can't believe you'd let Hale get away with killing those two vaqueros—and while they were getting back cattle Hale rustled from Don Ynocente."

"Wait a minute, Slocum." All trace of alcohol had burned from Stoudenmirer's speech. "What are you talking about? Who killed vaqueros? Where'd this happen?"

"Their names were Tomás and Jorge. Riders for Don Ynocente. They'd found a couple dozen head of cattle carrying the Ochoa brand that Hale had stashed on his spread.

Two of Hale's men gunned them down and then drove the herd over their corpses."

"You talk like you saw this."

"What do you think got Ynocente Ochoa so riled that he brought his men across the border?"

"You *saw* Hale murder these two Mexicans?"

"They were on Hale's ranch. What's it called?"

"The Circle H." Stoudenmirer stroked his mustache with his right index finger, thinking hard on what Slocum had said. "You witnessed it? You willing to testify in court?"

"I saw the vaqueros gunned down, but it might have been any of a big number of them doing the shooting. I didn't get that good a look at their faces."

"Murder to protect the illicit gain from rustling. I like that."

"Hale kidnapped—"

"Yeah, you told me. The Suarez girl. Think she might know who gunned down the Mexicans?"

Slocum saw that he had finally piqued Dallas Stoudenmirer's interest. The new marshal saw a way of breaking the Mannings' grip on El Paso, and doing it according to the law. If he could implicate them with Hale's men killing two Mexican cowboys, the entire town would be wide open again, and Stoudenmirer would run it unopposed.

Those were the thoughts Slocum saw reflected in Stoudenmirer's expression. The man might be a powerful good drinker, but as a card player he would be terrible.

"Bears looking into," the marshal said finally. "Since you were just leaving town, it won't make no never mind to you if we happen to be riding in the direction of the Circle H, will it?"

Slocum shook his head and smiled crookedly. Stoudenmirer had a way about him. "Not much out of my way," Slocum agreed.

"Let's ride, then."

They went out onto the boardwalk. The bodies of the

two men Stoudenmirer had shot down were still in the street. Stoudenmirer spat. "Damned deputies aren't doing their jobs. I told them to clean up after me. Damn. I'll have to see to this when I get back."

Stoudenmirer swung into the saddle of a large sorrel mare and impatiently motioned for Slocum to mount up. Slocum had to gallop to catch up with the marshal. Together they rode through El Paso. Slocum felt eyes watching them as they rode past. Stoudenmirer seemed to revel in the attention paid them. Slocum had an itchy feeling and waited for a hidden gunman to finish what had been started back at the saloon. He was relieved when they rode out of town and turned north toward the Hale ranch.

The road was little more than a double rutted dirt path, but Slocum enjoyed it. The day had turned cool again, as it sometimes did in the spring, but the threat of harsh summer clung to the air. Every time the clouds parted and let the full sun beat down, Slocum felt sweat beading up on his forehead.

"Your hat's got enough holes in it for summertime ventilation," Stoudenmirer observed. "You been doing all Don Ynocente's dirty work for free, or you getting paid?"

"Ynocente and I are old friends." Slocum stopped there. He didn't want to discuss their rustling days with a new marshal.

"Reckon you and him knew each other down San Antone way. Hell of a time a few years back. Rustle a bit on the Texas side of the river and get the beeves across into Mexico."

"Heard tell some people did that," Slocum allowed.

Stoudenmirer laughed. "You're a cool one. That Colt Navy of yours looks well used, too. Killed many men?"

"Only the nosy ones," said Slocum.

Stoudenmirer laughed even harder. "You're all right, Slocum, even if you do hang around with the likes of Ochoa."

Slocum let that ride, not wanting to anger Stoudenmirer.

The marshal seemed inclined to look into the deaths of two of Ynocente's men. It didn't matter that he did this for his own ends. Most lawmen wouldn't bother. Slocum tried to guess what Captain Baylor would have done if the murders had been reported to him. Although the Ranger captain had broken up the fight at Hale's corral and saved Slocum's hide, Slocum didn't for an instant think that the man did so out of any highfalutin sense of duty.

"This is the edge of Hale's spread," said Stoudenmirer, eyeing the empty expanse of desert. Thick tufts of grass grew in the bottoms of ravines where spring runoffs had provided enough water for fresh growth. Cattle would graze and cut it back, then move on. It might be weeks before the herds drifted back to graze on the new grass. From what he saw, Slocum guessed that Hale's cattle hadn't been along this road since the previous fall.

In the heat-hazy distance, Slocum saw a stand of gray-green salt cedar. From this and the brown, rugged slopes of the Franklin Mountains, he got his bearings. The saddle shape in the mountains provided a small pass that he used to home in on to gauge where Jorge and Tomás had been murdered.

"About there," Slocum said, pointing into the distance. "Maybe five miles. No more than that."

"The road to the main house is in that direction," Stoudenmirer said, getting his own bearing. "That's Anthony Gap up there, going across to Gadsden in New Mexico Territory. And where you're indicating ought to be right about where most of Hale's herd is grazing."

"You surely do know a lot about the area for just having arrived," said Slocum.

"I ask questions. Sometimes I get answers I like. When I don't. I beat it out of 'em. Amazing what else comes crushing out. One of Hale's boys got into trouble. I swear to God, he told me more about Johnny Hale than that scum-sucker's own mother knows."

"What happened to the cowboy?"

"Decided against staying in El Paso," Stoudenmirer said in a lugubrious tone. "Shame having the population drifting away like that, though nobody much gives a damn."

They rode in silence until they came to the top of the rise where Slocum had watched Hale and his men gun down the two vaqueros. Slocum dismounted and looked around the ground. He bent down and tried to make sense out of the tracks, but it was no use. The spring winds and the hot sun had worked to erase any mud and tracks he might have left to prove he'd been here.

"Down there, eh?" Stoudenmirer had remained on horseback. He urged his sorrel down the hill and meandered across the area. Slocum watched, at first thinking the man had finally reacted to all the liquor he had poured down his gullet. Stoudenmirer's path was erratic and sent him meandering around, but after a few minutes Slocum saw that the marshal criss-crossed the area thoroughly, using the sun to the best advantage to show him anything on the ground.

Slocum led his stallion down and into the middle of the grassy land where Jorge and Tomás had been killed. Stoudenmirer had already discovered a pair of silver conches the Mexicans used as fasteners for their leather vests. The marshal held them up. One had been mashed flat. The other was recognizable as having the Ochoa sigil on it.

"Don't prove a whole lot," Stoudenmirer said, "but it goes a ways towards making me believe you. This one's been stomped on something fierce. Looks like cow rather than horse. Steel shoes cut metal different from unshod cattle hooves." The marshal tucked both into his pocket and continued to walk around in his aimless way. He found a handful of spent brass.

"Don't go getting your hopes up, Slocum. There's other explanations for all this besides two vaqueros getting gunned down."

"How about this?" Slocum brushed away soft dirt and

sand and pulled out a tattered, big-brimmed sombrero. Blood had soaked one side and attracted ants.

"We're getting hotter. Need something definite, like a body or two."

Slocum didn't think Hale's men would drag the bodies far, and leaving them out under the desert sun would draw buzzards—and the circling scavengers would cause unwanted attention of anyone passing by.

"That stand of trees looks inviting," Slocum said. "Just the sort of place to bury a pair of bodies."

"I was thinking the same thing. Especially since this trial leads off in that direction." Stoudenmirer pointed out a faint path winding down to a sandy ravine bottom. Slocum bent and examined it, finding enough evidence to believe that the marshal was right. How Stoudenmirer had spotted this was beyond Slocum.

In the stand of trees it took only a cursory examination to find the graves. "You get on down to it. I'll watch. This way I'm not getting the evidence illegally."

Slocum failed to see how helping dig would affect evidence. "I dig if you promise to look into Consuela Suarez's kidnapping."

"Pushy bastard, aren't you?" Stoudenmirer settled down in the shade, a pint bottle of whiskey in hand. "Get on to digging and stop talking. Want a pull?" He held out the bottle for Slocum.

The fiery liquor burned all the way down into his belly. This helped Slocum get to work. In less than twenty minutes he had both vaqueros unearthed. Stoudenmirer looked down into the shallow graves.

"Yep," he said. "Both met untimely ends. By foul play is my official verdict. Now we have to find the criminals responsible for these heinous acts."

Slocum rubbed dirt off his hands onto his shirt as he looked back in the direction where the killings had occurred. A dust devil spun upward a hundred feet and more into the blue sky, but a smaller dust cloud caught his attention. He moved around so that he could shade his eyes from the sun. The dust cloud moved in a line opposite to that taken by the swirling dust devil.

"We got company coming," Slocum said.

"Good. I need to talk to a few of them about what I just found here." Stoudenmirer had finished going through the dead vaqueros' pockets. "Their murderers didn't leave much. Even went so far as to take the rest of those fancy silver conches with Ochoa's brand on them. Reckon I might be able to find who's got 'em in his pocket—and that this might be the same person who murdered poor Jorge and Tomás here?"

"There's at least five riders coming," said Slocum. He didn't have Stoudenmirer's low opinion of Hale's abilities. Five men meant five guns, and that spelled a passel of bullets flying in his direction.

"Tell you what, Slocum: I'll take the three on the left and you can have the two on the right. Seems like a fair deal?"

"Why do you get all the fun?" Slocum asked sarcastically. Then he was diving for cover. The approaching cowboys had sighted them and didn't even bother calling out a warning. The lead rider pulled his Winchester from its saddle sheath and opened fire.

The other riders followed with rounds from their sidearms.

"Doesn't look good," said Stoudenmirer. "They got us pinned down right proper." He pulled out his rifle and settled down, unconcerned. Slocum wondered if the alcohol had soaked the man's brain and destroyed important logical portions. Slocum preferred to be the attacker rather than the prey.

The odds were better. Lots better.

The whine of bullets over his head prompted Slocum to begin firing. His own rifle bucked and one rider jerked back in the saddle. The rider still lived, but might not be able to take part in the gunfight.

"You're damned good with that, Slocum," complimented Stoudenmirer. "We might actually ride out of here with all our parts intact. But there's one thing gnawing away at my innards that I got to ask you, seeing's how we might not make it."

"What's that?" Slocum sighted and squeezed off another round just to keep Hale's cowboys at a distance.

"You been down in Van Horn recently?"

"What?"

Stoudenmirer looked at him and grinned. "That's what I thought. You *did* shoot down that Ranger." Stoudenmirer rolled onto his belly, exposing his back to Slocum. "Figure the damned fool deserved it. You don't seem to be the kind who'd gun down a man unless he had it coming."

Slocum shook his head. This marshal was truly a puzzlement. Then he had more important things to occupy him. The four cowboys mounted a charge straight for the trees, riding hard behind a curtain of rifle bullets.

13

The bullets kicked up sand into Slocum's face. He spat, then tried to wipe his eyes clear. By the time he had succeeded, the riders were on top of him. A foot slipped free of a stirrup and kicked out hard, catching the muzzle of his rifle and knocking it from his hands. Behind him, he heard Dallas Stoudenmirer's bellygun roar. Why the marshal hadn't bothered to draw his more accurate Colt Slocum didn't know.

And he dared not take the time to find out. He had his hands full trying to stay alive.

A second rider tried to get his horse to rear and kick at Slocum. The low-hanging tree branches kept this from being effective. Slocum moved to his right, got his Colt Navy free, and aimed. Just as the mounted cowboy came into his sights, the world spun in crazy circles. Slocum thought the sun had gone down and the stars had come out when he wasn't looking.

"Got the son of a bitch," came hollow-ringing words from impossibly far away. Slocum shook his head and got his senses back. He didn't even remember dropping to his knees. Wiping some of the dirt from his Colt, he found an appropriate target and fired. The cowboy flew backward from his horse before he could backshot Stoudenmirer.

"Thanks, Slocum. That ought to hold them for a while."

"Yeah, right." Slocum forced himself to stand. He wobbled as he walked to where Stoudenmirer knelt beside the fallen cowhand.

"Damn, all he's got in his pocket is a pair of dimes. Don't Hale pay his men any better'n this? The wages of sin don't look to be as good as being marshal." Stoudenmirer spat. Slocum noticed that the marshal slid the two dimes into his vest pocket.

"Where did the other three go?" Slocum was still disoriented. One had struck him on the back of the head and raised a blood-oozing welt the shape of a rifle barrel.

"You surely didn't chase them off for me." The marshal's words carried a brittle sarcasm to them. "What do you think happened to them? They hightailed it when they saw who they were up against. No sane man faces down Dallas Stoudenmirer!"

Slocum stanched the flow of blood from the wound. His head had stopped spinning and leaving his body behind. Now everything around him dipped and dived and spun like a dust devil.

"What do we do? They rode to get Hale. Won't take him long to have a dozen men out here," said Slocum.

"Let 'im come. I got questions to ask him."

"You got a death wish?" Slocum hardly believed his ears. "He's going to come and find those—" Slocum pointed at the two vaqueros' corpses. "And he's going to kill us, too. No witnesses to a crime are better than two."

"He's up against the duly appointed law in El Paso," Stoudenmirer said, as if this settled everything. "Hale's not got the sense God gave a mule, but he's not so stupid as to try killing me."

"Four of his men just tried."

"They didn't like your looks."

Slocum wondered if Stoudenmirer had ridden without his hat and got a touch of sunstroke. Something had addled the man's brains if he thought for an instant that Johnny Hale wasn't capable of killing them both and laughing while he did it.

"Let's go back into El Paso and fetch a couple of your deputies. We need firepower out here."

"They got even fewer brains than Hale. Too much firepower along with too little smarts means people die needlessly."

"Do you want me to go back?" asked Slocum.

"Turn tail and run, if it suits you. Don't make no never mind to me. I'm letting the killers come to me. It's too taxing to do it any other way. Who do you think will come ridin' up with Hale? Murderers always got to know if anyone suspects them. Whoever done it will be with that pile of donkey dung, mark my words."

Slocum retrieved his rifle and cleaned it off, making sure that it chambered shells properly. Without a word he mounted his stallion and rode off in the direction of town. He had just got out of the marshal's sight, though, when he wheeled his horse around and circled to come up from the far side of the copse. The trees shielded him from Stoudenmirer and the rise afforded him a good view of the surrounding countryside. He figured that Hale would come riding up a deep ravine that ran in the proper direction, mostly out of sight from here, but Slocum would still have ample warning.

He settled down and pulled the fixings of a cigarette from his pocket. He carefully built his smoke and searched until he found the small metal tube with his lucifers. He unscrewed the cap and pulled out a bulbous-headed stick and lit it. The smoked gusting down into his lungs relaxed him and made him forget all about the aches and pains he had picked up like burrs under a saddle blanket.

Now and then he checked the direction of the wind to be sure he didn't alert Stoudenmirer to his presence. The wind blew in his face, carrying the smoke away from the marshal's post down in the small grove of trees.

Slocum thought hard about Stoudenmirer. The man seemed to be suicidal, not caring about the odds he faced. Slocum needed him to get to Consuela. Without the marshal's help, he wasn't sure he could ever find the woman and rescue her. He spat out the last shreds of tobacco left from the cigarette and wondered if he would ever find the lovely Consuela even *with* Stoudenmirer's help.

He considered riding over to the Hale ranch house while Johnny and his men came here. Slocum didn't think Hale would be stupid enough to keep Consuela there, though. Truth to tell, Slocum had no good idea how to find Consuela short of catching Hale and torturing the information from him.

If he wanted to get his hands on Hale, the best he could do was wait for Hale to come riding up—as he had to, sooner or later.

Slocum smiled crookedly. He worried a different problem like a hound dog with a bone and came to the same conclusion Stoudenmirer had: let Hale come to them.

The sound of approaching riders alerted him. Slocum fell belly-down on the top of the hill and got his Winchester into position. This was the kind of fight he did best. All the training the Confederacy had afforded him came into play. He watched Hale and four others come up and out of the arroyo he had already figured they'd be in. They fanned out to make it harder for a missed shot on one to take out another.

Slocum didn't care about that. They were all sitting ducks. He held back squeezing the trigger until he got some inkling about Stoudenmirer's plan. Even though he didn't really believe it, Slocum had to admit that Stoudenmirer might try to make a deal with Hale. Captain Baylor was known for taking money to smooth over small breaches of the public peace. What was Stoudenmirer's price?

"That you in there, Stoudenmirer?" called Hale. "Git on out here where we can see you."

Dallas Stoudenmirer strode out, thumbs hooked into his britches. "Good to see you again, Johnny. I was getting tired of waiting for you to get here."

"Where's the other one with you?"

"He took off for town. Didn't want to stay and see a lawman do his job."

"What do you mean?"

Slocum watched the reactions of the men with Hale. Two of them looked jumpier than long-tailed cats sitting by a rocking chair.

"I came out here to do some arresting. Seems like your boys done up and killed two Mexicans. Found their bodies in there. Didn't even given them a decent burial."

"For a greaser?" One of the pair Slocum suspected spat. "You come all the way out here to bother about them?"

"Murder's a crime in these here United States."

"Let the Texas Rangers deal with it," said Hale, leaning forward in the saddle.

"I reckon that means you got Captain Baylor bought off good and proper. Tell me how much a Ranger captain's bribe is these days. I'm always curious about such matters."

The man at the far end of the line went for his gun. Slocum lined up his rifle sights and squeezed off an easy shot. The report echoed across the desert long after the thud of the cowboy's body hitting the ground had died out.

All eyes turned toward the hill where Slocum perched. Slocum noticed that Stoudenmirer's mustache twitched as the marshal smiled. He had his own Colt out and firing. A second man jerked back and slumped to the side, falling from his horse.

"Johnny, don't do doing anything that will get yourself killed," Stoudenmirer said. "Though Heaven knows I'd love to plug your ugly carcass with a few rounds."

"How, many men you got lurking up there, Stoudenmirer?" demanded Hale. "You're trespassing on private land. You and all your henchmen!"

"Not exactly. You claim this for your spread but it's my official judgment that we're standing on open range country."

"You won't get away with this, Marshal."

"Reckon it puts you in a better position if it *is* open range. Otherwise, I got to take you in, too, if two murders happened on your property. If'n this is open range, I need only find the culprits responsible for killing poor Tomás and Jorge back there."

Slocum saw Hale's face contort as he considered what the marshal said. He finally said, "This might not be as close to my property as I thought."

"Johnny, you're not—" One of the cowboys saw what his boss was doing and didn't like it. Hale was going to hand over to the marshal the two responsible for the vaqueros' deaths. Slocum was amazed at the power Stoudenmirer carried with him. Sheer brashness backed down Hale on his own land.

"These two the ones who done the dirty deed?" Stoudenmirer asked.

"You're not turning us over to the law!" cried one. He bent low over his horse's neck and tried to run. Slocum's accurate shooting winged him and knocked him from the saddle. The other cowboy went for his gun and started firing wildly.

"You'll never lock me up in that miserable jail!" he shouted. He tried to gun down his boss, but Hale was already spurring his horse forward.

Slocum tried to get a good shot at the fleeing man but missed twice. If anything, his shots only added speed to the fleeing killer. Slocum cursed and got onto his stallion. He trotted downhill to where Stoudenmirer lifted up the one injured cowboy and shook the man hard enough to rattle his teeth.

"Tell me about it, scum. Tell me all about how you shot down the Mexicans and then ran the beeves over them to hide it."

"No, you'll never get me to talk. You can't hang me for killin' a damned Mexican!"

"You killed a man. You're going to answer for that."

"Prove it!"

Slocum stared down from horseback at the man. Stoudenmirer went through the fallen man's pockets, pulled out a silver conch, and held it up. The way the cowboy's face went pasty white confirmed that this was one killer.

"You even robbed him, you son of a bitch. I found trampled conches with Ochoa's brand on them near where you shot them down."

"No, it wasn't me."

Slocum lifted his rifle and covered Hale. "Better not think on putting him out of his misery." Hale's hand had snaked toward his pistol. When he saw how steady Slocum's hand was, he backed down.

"Wasn't thinking of anything like that. You just keep your yap shut, Stevenson," he told the man on the ground. "We'll get you a lawyer and see what case the marshal's got against you. Ain't no white jury's ever gonna find you guilty."

"You talk a good game, Hale. You're lucky you're not going to trial with him." Slocum stood in his stirrups looking for the dust cloud that marked the other murderer's getaway. It wasn't hard to see. Slocum had a good idea where he was heading and how to stop him.

He asked Stoudenmirer, "Did you know I was up there on the hill?"

"Figured you might be. You're not the kind to go off and let another fellow have all the fun."

"You could have been killed if I hadn't been there."

Stoudenmirer stroked his mustache. "Reckon you're right. Never thought of that." He laughed, deep and long. "You want to go get that other fellow?"

"Why me?"

"I can always deputize you and make it legal."

"Wouldn't like that," said Slocum. To Hale he said, "What's the cowboy's name? The one that's halfway to Mexico by now."

"Peveler."

"Stevenson and Peveler. What a sweet pair you make," said Stoudenmirer. "And how good you're gonna look dangling side by side when we hang you."

Slocum noted that Stoudenmirer spoke not for the prisoner's benefit but for Johnny Hale's. The marshal tormented the man, goading him into action. Hale's hand twitched again, but the sight of Stoudenmirer standing ready to shoot at the slightest hint of trouble took the starch out of Hale.

"You won't get by with this, Stoudenmirer. I got friends."

"Yeah, I suppose you do. Why don't you give Doc and Frank my regards? Maybe you can even invite them to the hanging after we run these two up before Judge Magoffin."

Hale's face turned fiery red. He jerked savagely on his horse's reins and galloped off.

"Why let him go?" demanded Slocum, when Stoudenmirer reached up and grabbed the rifle to keep him from putting a bullet in the middle of Hale's spine.

"He'll suffer more if I take his men away from him, one by one. Like this puddle of scum." Stoudenmirer kicked Stevenson. The man went for a pistol on the ground. Stoudenmirer took two quick steps and kicked again, this time the toe of his boot connecting squarely with Stevenson's chin. The man's head snapped back and he sank to the ground, unconscious.

"Get on after what's his name—Peveler. Go on now, or you won't have any fun a'tall today."

Slocum looked at the marshal, wondering what twisted mind worked inside that skull. "You know I'll bring him back to stand trial, don't you?"

"Yep. I figured I might enjoy killing him too much if I went. This way I get a clean sweep of killers. Be sure that he's got some good evidence on him when you catch him."

"He's a killer. I won't need to plant evidence on him."

"Do it your way, then, though it seems a mite inefficient," Stoudenmirer said, frowning. "Just as long as you get to it before he hightails it all the way to Canada."

Slocum wheeled his horse around and started after Peveler. He didn't have to push the stallion. He had studied the lay of the land and decided how Peveler would ride. The cowboy knew that going to the ranch house wouldn't gain him spit. He'd go due north, catch a road across Anthony Gap, and end up over in New Mexico Territory, beyond Marshal Stoudenmirer's authority. There was only one problem with this.

Slocum had a faster route and could cut off Peveler's escape. Slocum had no need to try to hide. Peveler didn't want to give away his position if Stoudenmirer had brought a posse with him. Slocum cut across the Circle H, scaring a few strays from the main herd. Riding harder, he got up a rise and peered down across a sandy stretch of desert populated more with snakes and lizards than humans.

Slocum spotted his prey instantly. Just as he had thought, Peveler was headed for the safety of New Mexico. From there, he could go anywhere—north to Las Vegas, west to Tucson, northwest to Salt Lake City. He might even go north a ways and double back into Texas, providing he had nothing to fear from Captain Baylor and the Rangers.

Putting spurs to his black stallion's flanks, he rode to intercept the fleeing killer. Slocum thought about the marshal as he rode. The man was as crazy as a loon. He had to be to face down half a dozen armed men, banking on Slocum being up on the hill to cover him. Still, gold badge and all, Stoudenmirer had a style about him that Slocum admired. There weren't too many lawmen who adhered to the law or even their own personal view of it like Stoudenmirer. The man didn't seem corruptible, leastways not like Baylor or George Campbell.

Peveler glanced over his shoulder and saw Slocum coming up fast behind. The man urged his horse to greater speed but the animal was tired out from the sandy bottoms of the arroyos they'd been travelling. Slocum steadily closed the distance between them.

When he got close enough to see the whites of Peveler's wide, frightened eyes, Slocum decided how best to proceed. An easy shot would bring the fleeing murderer down. Even as he considered it, he realized how shrewd Stoudenmirer had been. Consuela Suarez was still held hostage somewhere by Johnny Hale. Stevenson and Peveler together might be able to wrangle a deal and escape the hangman's noose if they turned Hale in for kidnapping.

Slocum found the lariat bouncing on the right side of his saddle. He quickly unfastened it and worked a loop open. An expert toss landed the rope around Peveler. Slocum's horse dug in its heels and Slocum looped the rope around the saddle horn. Peveler flew from the saddle, landing hard enough to knock the wind out of him.

Slocum dismounted and took the man's pistol from his belt.

"There some good reason I shouldn't leave your carcass out here for the vultures?" Slocum asked.

"Do what you want." Peveler fought to regain his wind.

"Where's Consuela being held?"

Peveler spat at Slocum and instantly regretted it. Slocum snapped the rope around the man's shoulders, signalling his horse to back up. Peveler was dragged a few feet before Slocum caught up and stopped the horse.

"Be like that," he said, mounting. Slocum reined the stallion around and took off at a brisk pace to rejoin Stoudenmirer. He didn't much care if Peveler kept up or not. The captive cowboy might get himself dragged along for a few miles or run along just fine. As long as he kept his lips sealed concerning Consuela, Slocum didn't much give a damn what happened to him.

14

"No!" shouted Ynocente Ochoa. "We must get Consuela back. We dare not let her stay in that swine's grip!"

"We both know Hale has her stashed somewhere. Finding her is damned near impossible, though."

"No, Slocum, not when I begin work on him." The feral flash in Don Ynocente's eyes told Slocum what the man meant. Ynocente had been good with a knife when they had rustled cattle. Slocum had no reason to believe that he had lost any skill over the years.

"Let's see if Stoudenmirer's plan works."

"I do not trust this new marshal," Pedro Suarez spoke up. Ochoa's foreman was heavily bandaged and walked slowly, favoring his injured right side. They went to the courthouse set back from the street. El Paso's citizenry had gathered for the big trial and the crowd outside the whitewashed building was respectable in size.

"I'm not sure I trust him much, either," admitted Slocum. He had tried repeatedly to figure out Stoudenmirer's angle. The man had a real grudge against Johnny Hale and bringing Stevenson and Peveler to trial was the marshal's way of making Hale suffer a mite. Through Hale, Stoudenmirer got to the Manning brothers. And from the few things the marshal said, he had no love for the Texas Rangers in general or Captain Baylor in particular.

Slocum took off his hat and brushed the dust from it.

Stoudenmirer had known who shot down the Ranger in Van Horn and had done nothing about it. It wasn't because Slocum was a friend or that he believed the Ranger might really have deserved what he got. He was letting Slocum off scot free because of a powerful hatred.

Slocum didn't care squat about that. He wanted Consuela back. The thought of the lovely woman being held captive by the likes of Hale made his blood start to boil. Ynocente's wrath was huge; Slocum wasn't sure that his own anger didn't reach even greater heights. But there was so little they could do unless they learned where the girl was being held. If the trial looked as if it went against the two cowboys, they might tell what they knew. From there, Slocum didn't worry what Stoudenmirer's game was. He'd play that hand himself.

There would be even more dead men when he finished.

"The gringo judges are all crooked," said Pedro. "They do not care if we die. They do not care if innocent girls are stolen away. These two men will walk from the court free men."

"They won't," said Slocum in a tone that caused both Ynocente and Suarez to look at him.

Ynocente slapped him on the back and said, "There *is* much of the old Slocum I rode with in you. I'd thought it had melted like snow in the spring sun."

"I'll get Consuela back," he said, wondering who he was promising this to. Not for the first time, he thought Ynocente Ochoa was more concerned over the girl's safety than Pedro was. Ynocente was *patrón* and responsible for the welfare of those who worked for him, but his emotions ran deeper.

"I do not like this building," said Ynocente, staring at the entryway with distaste. "They make us give over our weapons." Stoudenmirer's deputies took everyone's guns and stashed them in a small cloakroom before letting the noisy crowd into the courtroom. Slocum surrendered his ebony-handled Colt without protest; he still carried a derringer in his boot top. He wondered how many others in the room were similarly armed. Still, the intent to keep peace was obvious.

"How many vaqueros did you bring with you?" Slocum asked Ynocente.

"Ten. Too many more would have provoked the people of El Paso. Fewer would have been dangerous. I do not trust anyone on this side of the river."

Slocum said nothing to this. Ynocente had little reason to. Hale—and behind him, Frank and Doc Manning—had brought a world of hurt to the Mexican rancher.

"There, that one. The marshal. I see a pistol stuck inside his shirt," said Pedro, pointing to George Campbell.

"He's the former marshal, and he's drunker than a stewed hoot owl. Don't worry about him," said Slocum. But the way Campbell glared at them made Slocum uneasy. The deputies had not done a good job enforcing the court order to keep firearms out if they let a drunken sot like this in with a Colt shoved under his shirt.

"The two who killed Jorge and Tomás, where are they?" asked Ynocente. "I do not see them."

Slocum didn't see either Peveler or Stevenson in the court. He rose and went to Stoudenmirer. Slocum ignored the odor of whiskey on the marshal as he asked, "Where are the defendants?"

"Good morning, Slocum. Pretty day for a trial, ain't it?"

The expression on Stoudenmirer's face was unreadable. "Where are they?" Slocum repeated.

"Seems I couldn't get Magoffin to sit on this case," Stoudenmirer said after a spell. "He's got it into his head that being judge and alderman don't mix."

"So?"

"Judge Buckler's a special friend of Doc Manning, if you get my drift."

"The judge released them." Slocum's words were flat and emotionless.

"Don't go getting your bowels in an uproar, Slocum. He

released them and they decided not to show up for the trial, but they're going to be tried no matter what. Might be better not having them around to cloud the issue."

Slocum didn't see it that way. Peveler and Stevenson were going to be set free.

"Don Ynocente isn't going to like this," said Slocum.

"Ochoa's going to have to learn that this is the way some things are. Maybe we can smooth things over with him. I'll work on it."

Slocum frowned. Stoudenmirer was taking the two men's release too easily. Stoudenmirer played a bigger game, and Slocum didn't know what it was. The marshal had never had real interest in Peveler and Stevenson as killers. He had rousted the men to get back at Johnny Hale. Or was there more to it? Slocum got a queasy feeling in his gut that Stoudenmirer worked all ends against the middle —and that was exactly where Slocum stood. No matter which way he turned, he was going to be in deep trouble.

"Shh," said Stoudenmirer. "Witnesses are getting ready to testify."

Slocum went back and sat beside Ynocente and Pedro Suarez. He could not believe his ears. The "witnesses" all testified to the fine character of the accused, how Chris Peveler and Frank Stevenson were salt of the earth and would never think of killing any damned greasers.

"Wait, Ynocente." Slocum had to restrain the Mexican to keep him from leaving and getting his vaqueros. They would tear El Paso apart. "This isn't what I bargained for. Stoudenmirer's up to something. Let's see what it is."

"Consuela is still in their hands. I will not tolerate this . . . this mockery of justice! It is not enough that Jorge and Tomás were slaughtered like animals! Now we must sit through this travesty as if it meant something!"

"Order in the court!" Judge Buckler rapped the butt end of his pistol on the table. "I think we've heard enough. There's no question in my mind as to the innocence of the two defendants. I order them released, wherever they are."

Ynocente Ochoa shot to his feet. Slocum kept him from angrily shouting at the judge.

Buckler looked up and saw the fury in Ynocente's face. The smile on the judge's face was more infuriating than anything else he had done in the courtroom. "If there's no other business, I'll order the bodies released to you, Don Ynocente. Unless you got something you want to say to the court."

"Their bodies, Don Ynocente. We can bury them properly," said Pedro.

"Causing trouble now isn't going to rescue Consuela, either," said Slocum. "I promised you I'd find her. I'm sorry about this, but I *will* find her. I've never broken my word."

"I know that, John." Ynocente jerked his arm free of Slocum's grip and motioned for Suarez to join them.

"Court's adjourned." The judge rapped his pistol butt smartly. "Let's all go down to Frank Manning's saloon and have a drink. This is thirsty business."

Stoudenmirer stopped by Slocum and said, "You joining the court in a drink?"

"I wouldn't drink with them so that I could spit on the judge," said Slocum.

"Don't go getting yourself all riled for nothing, Slocum. This will work out. Believe it." Stoudenmirer started from the courtroom, stopped, and said, "Better check your pistol before you get out in the street. There might be some unpleasantness after this."

Slocum hurried after Stoudenmirer. The marshal touched the bulge in his left coat pocket and then checked the heavy Colt hanging in the cross-draw holster at his right hip. Satisfied, he went out into the El Paso streets.

"We will get their bodies home," said Don Ynocente.

"What?" Slocum looked at his friend. "Sorry. I was thinking about other things." He watched as Stoudenmirer mounted and rode toward the center of town. The marshal didn't seem to have a care in the world, yet Slocum had the feeling all hell was about to break loose.

"You wish for us to stay? Will this help you getting back Consuela?" Ynocente's eagerness was almost pathetic.

"You might leave me one or two men, but it's for the best if you get on back to Mexico. There's nothing more that can be done right now."

"Lopez will stay with you." Slocum eyed the vaquero Ynocente had chosen. The scars on his face showed he had been in too many knife fights—and had lost most of them. The heavy pistol shoved into his waistband had seen better days, but the man's demeanor showed that he might be handy to have around.

Slocum nodded, then said, "This is all going to be settled real soon, Ynocente."

"It will be. By noon tomorrow it will be or all El Paso will be burned to the ground. Juan has agreed. The army will back us if we come across to find Consuela." Ynocente turned even grimmer. "If she has been harmed, there will not be a gringo left alive in this town."

Ochoa spun and stalked off. Slocum wondered where that put him. He decided he didn't want to know. Ynocente's anger was not to be contained much longer. Slocum knew that only his persuasion and old friendship had prevented the rancher from doing anything desperate before now.

Slocum watched the Mexicans ride back to Paso del Norte, wondering if he had done right in convincing Ynocente to do nothing. The threat of an invasion might have shaken the citizens of El Paso enough to bring Consuela's kidnappers to justice.

Slocum snorted. The only justice likely to be meted out in this town hung in the holster at his hip. The Texas Rangers might be as crooked as the Mannings. Captain Baylor surely did ride along with them, if not in cahoots, then in spirit. The trial had been a mockery. Peveler and

Stevenson were only a part of the whole rotten mess starting to boil in El Paso.

A blood feud might clear the air. It would also fill the Concordia Cemetery all the way out to Hueco Tanks and the Butterfield Stage station.

Slocum mounted and rode slowly, his keen eyes studying the people along the streets. Tension mounted. Stoudenmirer had been right when he said that caution was better than headlong confrontation.

"*Señor* Slocum," said Lopez, "what is it we do?"

"We go and get a drink. We wait. We keep our ears open and see if we can't find where Peveler and Stevenson are. They know where Hale's keeping Consuela. I'm sure of it. That's why they were afraid to appear in court."

"*Sí,* yes, I would have made them talk," Lopez said, smiling wickedly as he flashed a thick-bladed knife. "They would talk much—before they died."

The Ben Dowell Saloon was the most boisterous along the street. Slocum dismounted and tethered his stallion. He motioned for Lopez to stay outside while he checked the goings-on inside.

Slocum got to the middle of the street when he heard George Campbell's whining, drunken voice. "Any American that's a friend of Mexicans ought to be hanged!"

Slocum's hand moved to his Colt, thinking Campbell meant him. But the former marshal stood in the saloon door, his back to the street. Whoever he yelled at was inside.

Campbell grunted and came staggering back to sit heavily in the dusty street. Slocum moved back, ready for anything. Marshal Stoudenmirer came out of the saloon, fire in his eyes and a half-empty whiskey bottle in his right hand.

"No man says what you just did and lives to tell about it. I enforce the laws in El Paso. *All* the laws, unlike the former marshal, you drunken son of a bitch."

"You think more of them than you do of your own kind!" accused Campbell, getting to his feet. Slocum was hard pressed to tell who was drunker. Stoudenmirer took a deep draught from the bottle and threw it aside. Campbell weaved on his feet.

"You been asking for trouble ever since I blew into town," said Stoudenmirer. "Let's see how much of a man you are."

"More'n you'll ever be!" Campbell cried.

Campbell's bravado puzzled Slocum. He didn't have the man pegged for much in the way of backbone. Slocum took his eyes off Campbell and looked up and down the street. Coming around the side of the saloon were three men, all carrying rifles. Slocum recognized Johnny Hale immediately. It took several seconds before he realized that Peveler and Stevenson were the cowboys with him. Campbell was setting up the marshal for a drygulching.

"Stoudenmirer!" Slocum shouted. "To your left!" Slocum had his pistol out and firing. His warning had also alerted Hale and his henchmen. They dived for cover and opened fire.

The street filled with leaden death. Slocum twisted and dived for the walk behind him. He hit the boards hard enough to knock a few planks loose. He kept rolling, splinters flying all around him. Whoever fired wasn't a good shot—and for that Slocum thanked his lucky stars. He rolled again and came up behind a rain barrel beside a store. The barrel was almost empty, but provided enough cover for him to reload his Colt.

By the time he looked up he was staring down the barrel of a rifle. Hale smiled, his lips curled back in a feral snarl. "So long, sucker," the rancher said, his finger tightening on the trigger.

Slocum worked to get the cylinder back into his Colt, but he knew death had found him at last. He jerked when the report came. For a second he wondered why death didn't hurt more. He had been wounded many times and there had always been sharp, burning pain with the bullet's entry. Not now.

It took him a second to realize that Johnny Hale was the one who lay dead on the dusty ground. Slocum poked his head around the barrel and saw Dallas Stoudenmirer wave, a broad grin splitting the man's face.

"You can return the favor sometime, Slocum," the marshal called.

"I warned you about Hale in the first place. What more do you want?"

"Hell, I knew they were there!"

Stoudenmirer cut off the yammering and started firing again. Chris Peveler had tried for a quick shot at Stoudenmirer's head and had missed. Peveler grunted and staggered back when the marshal's return fire found a target. Slocum saw that the man was just scratched. He tried to make the injury more permanent. All he succeeded in doing was driving Peveler and Stevenson back toward the stables.

He reloaded and moved into the street. A strange, unnatural calm had settled. He looked around and saw timid townspeople peering through windows.

"Reckon this hoo-haw is about over," said the marshal. He knocked the spent brass from his pistol and reloaded. All signs of drunkenness had passed.

"You got both Campbell and Hale," said Slocum. He glanced over his shoulder and saw another casualty of the fight. Lopez lay curled up next to his horse. Slocum went and checked the vaquero. A bullet had caught him square in the head.

"At least he didn't linger. I saw a gutshot man who took damned near a month to die," said Stoudenmirer. "Him dying like this makes it a bit touchier with Don Ynocente, though, doesn't it?"

"Reckon it does. Ynocente put Lopez here to protect me. Too bad I wasn't able to keep him from getting his head blown off."

Stoudenmirer shrugged. "Leastways, I got rid of part of

my trouble." He indicated Hale lying face down in the dust. "Not that I'll miss ole George Campbell none."

Slocum heard the heavy pounding of horses' hooves as Peveler and Frank Stevenson beat it out of town. He thrust the Colt Navy into its holster and turned without saying a word to Stoudenmirer. The marshal had got what he wanted. Johnny Hale was gone and his former rival was dead, too.

That did nothing to rescue Consuela Suarez. Slocum decided that the time for being law-abiding and following Marshal Stoudenmirer's lead was past. The two men riding out of El Paso were his only chances of finding Consuela.

Slocum hoped he wasn't too late.

15

"Are you going after them?" Slocum demanded.

"Got things to do here in town," said Stoudenmirer. "Mighty thirsty work, yes, sir, it is." He cocked his head to one side and stared at the fallen Lopez. "Don't reckon you want to deal with that?"

"Send a deputy to tell Ochoa," said Slocum. He knew what was happening. Stoudenmirer wanted him to do his dirty work for him—and Slocum was willing.

"I doubt there's one what would cross the Rio Grande for that, but one can be sent. I got to go keep a watch out for the Mannings."

Slocum hesitated when he saw Dallas Stoudenmirer going back into the Ben Dowell Saloon. "Why there?" Slocum called.

Stoudenmirer's eyebrows rose in surprise. "You didn't know? Frank's leased this here place. Might carry another man's name on it, but the stench of the Manning boys is everywhere. What better place to sit and wait for them to surface?"

"They will," said Slocum, looking at Hale's cadaver gathering flies in the hot El Paso sun.

Stoudenmirer smiled. "Give Peveler and Stevenson hell for me." With that, the marshal went off whistling.

The swinging doors had hardly stopped moving when Slocum was mounted and riding out of town. He trotted along until he got to the outskirts, then slowed to study the ground. The sun-baked land carried few hoofprints, but he found a new set of tracks leading north. He didn't think the two cowboys would return directly to the Circle H. They wouldn't want to bring back the bad news of Johnny Hale getting himself blown away by the marshal. More likely they'd see their protection gone along with Hale and would hightail it for New Mexico Territory, as Chris Peveler had tried once before when Slocum had ridden him down.

Slocum urged his stallion to more speed and kept his eyes peeled for any change in the trail. Crossing tracks confused him now and then, often making him get down and study the prints closely. He kept after the freshest tracks until they cut suddenly toward the east. Slocum tried to make sense out of that.

Why go deeper into Texas? If Stoudenmirer put out a warrant for their arrest, this made them fair game for the Texas Rangers.

The name echoed in his head like a cannon blast. Texas Ranger. Captain Baylor. Hale had been a pawn of the Manning brothers. Slocum knew that for certain, but could the rancher have been working for yet another master? The Rangers had a reputation for being tough on rustlers and horse thieves, but Hale had worked openly and with no interference from the law until Marshal Stoudenmirer got his gold badge pinned on his chest.

Baylor would do anything for a quick dollar. That reputation had circulated so widely that Slocum had heard it in half a dozen places in West Texas. El Paso was hardly the center of the universe. Slocum smiled slightly. He had seen an editorial in the *Las Vegas Optic* that said El Paso was the jumping-off place of creation and the worst hole in the Southwest. That made the town ideal for someone with a big greed like Baylor.

Slocum had heard that the whores charged union rates of fifty cents but that some bagnios charged more because of overhead from payoffs to the law. He hadn't had time to find out for himself, he thought ruefully. But then, he had found Consuela Suarez, and she was worlds better than any four-bit whore.

Slocum tensed up inside when he thought of the girl, still a captive. At least, he hoped she was still a prisoner. The thought of her dead body lying out in the hot sun and drawing a flock of vultures made him so mad that he could hardly stand it.

"I'll find you, you sons of bitches," he promised Peveler and Stevenson. "You might get off scot free on killing those vaqueros, but you won't get away with kidnapping Consuela."

Slocum followed the solitary trail toward Hueco Tanks and the stage station, wondering if the two cowboys intended to get on the Butterfield stage and vanish into parts unknown. If they tried, he would pursue. He had no other way of finding where they'd hidden Consuela.

Again the trail doglegged toward the south. Slocum worried that they led him on a wild goose chase—or worse. He might be on the wrong trail. The sand kept tracks for only a few hours at the most, minutes if a storm whipped up. He was lucky in that the spring winds were quiet today. A full-fledged dust storm would destroy any chance he had for finding the two.

When he saw a narrow, rutted alkali-dust road and a sign announcing to the world that this was the Marsh Ranch, Slocum reined in and thought on this. He had heard the name before. It took several seconds before it came to him. George Campbell had said that the Texas Rangers were being quartered here.

Slocum knew now that he had to fight off not only the remnants of Hale's gang of rustlers but the entire might of the Rangers. Captain Baylor wouldn't take long to decide that Slocum was responsible for killing the Ranger in Van Horn, simply because it was an easy way to get rid of a nuisance. That it was true had nothing to do with what Baylor would claim.

Slocum knew better than to ride on in. He wondered if he had been careless already. Baylor wasn't the kind of man to leave much to chance. Not even greed would get in the way of his own continued survival. Sentries posted around the ranch would keep watch and mounted patrols might sweep through the area to keep out unwanted visitors.

Like John Slocum.

Riding along the road showed no sign of surveillance. Slocum cut off and rode over the sandy dunes. The range-land here would provide sparse grass for cattle, though he thought that adequate water might give decent irrigated cropland. Slocum dismounted and walked to the top of a large dune. From the vantage point he stared into the sun in the west, hoping to catch sight of the ranch house and be able to get in and out under cover of darkness.

He saw a pair of riders—and they spotted him immediately. Slocum cursed when he saw one jerk around and point in his direction. He looked down and saw that the watch chain dangling from his vest had reflected light and betrayed him. He swung over the crest of the dune and slid down to mount. Choosing a direction to ride proved hard. The two sentries would expect him to ride hell-bent for leather away. The wind had cut a shallow canyon in the sand dunes so that either a north or south route looked most promising.

Slocum urged his black stallion back up the slope and waited just behind the wind-rippled crest. He heard the hoofbeats as the riders split and circled the dune, one going south and the other north to cut off any escape.

He waited until they came around the distant ends and then got his horse over the top and down. Separated as the riders were, he could choose which one he wanted to eliminate. He went south and rode straight up to the startled Ranger.

"Who?" the Texas Ranger started. That was as far as he got. Slocum put the spurs to his horse and galloped by, swinging his lariat as he went. The rope caught the Ranger square across the chest and sent him tumbling to the ground. Even over the pounding of his horse's hooves, Slocum heard the air gusting out of the Ranger's lungs. He reined in, spun, and went back. The lawman struggled to sit up. Slocum dropped a loop of rope around him and tightened. The Ranger got to his feet and inadvertently let Slocum add another loop, this one around his legs. Slocum jerked hard and the man fell to the sandy ground hard enough to knock the wind from him again. Slocum dismounted and finished the hogtying.

By the time he had the Ranger trussed up, the man was fuming mad and shouting. "I'll have your hide for this!" he hollered. Slocum pulled off the Ranger's bandana and stuffed it into his mouth, shutting off further outcries. He took the lawman's gun and heaved it over a dune, completing the capture.

The Ranger struggled and kicked, but Slocum had done his work too well for easy escape. Slocum went hunting for the other Texas Ranger and found him within minutes.

This time he wasn't as lucky and the Ranger wasn't taken by surprise.

"Son of a bitch!" the Ranger swore, pulling out his six-shooter.

Slocum ducked under a pair of bullets meant to take the top off his head. Slocum bent far forward, hugging his horse's neck to give as small a target as possible. He urged the stallion away to a spot where he was able to tumble from horseback and get behind scattered mesquite on the edge of an arroyo.

"You're not going to come snoopin' around here and get away with it!" the Texas Ranger warned. Slocum knew the man shouted all this to build his own courage and to sap Slocum's. Not answering put questions in the man's mind —and doubt might make him curious and careless.

"Surrender. I'm a Texas Ranger. You ain't gonna leave here alive, 'less you do give up."

Slocum began moving, letting the Ranger keep up his tirade. Slocum scrambled up a sandy, crumbling arroyo embankment and fell flat on his belly. He didn't have a good shot at the lawman from here, but he was protected and the Ranger wasn't.

Slocum couldn't believe his good luck. The Texas Ranger got his horse down into the arroyo and galloped forward, bullets flying everywhere. When the lawman rode past, Slocum acted. He got his feet under him and launched himself through the air. His attack missed hitting the Ranger directly, but Slocum's left arm snaked around the rider's neck and both men tumbled to the sandy arroyo bottom. Slocum ended up on top of the heap.

He cocked his Colt and aimed it between the Ranger's eyes. "Move and I'll blow your head off," Slocum said. His voice was cold and carried no bravado, only the promise of swift death.

"You're stirring up a den of rattlers, mister," the Ranger said. Slocum saw fear in the man's eyes, but he hid it well. "You're not going to get away with it."

"With what?"

"Whatever you're up to. Nobody comes ridin' out here 'less they got something illegal on their minds."

"The wicked flee when no man pursues," Slocum quoted.

"What?"

"You part of the gang Captain Baylor's put together to rustle cattle over in Mexico?"

The man's eyes widened in surprise. Slocum saw that he was as guilty as sin.

"I don't give a good goddamn about that," Slocum said. "I want Peveler and Stevenson."

"Those two owlhoots? What's so special about them?"

"They know about Consuela Suarez's kidnapping." Again Slocum got a startled reaction from the Ranger— and Slocum knew he'd struck pay dirt. "You know about her kidnapping, too," Slocum said. "Where are they holding her prisoner?"

"You ain't gettin' a damned thing from me, mister. Captain Baylor'd have my hide for talking."

"That's all right, because I'm going to have it if you *don't* talk." Slocum saw that fear of and maybe even loyalty to the Ranger captain would keep his prisoner from talking. Slocum reached down, grabbed a handful of shirt, and pulled the Ranger to his feet.

"Start walking," Slocum said.

"You can't—"

Slocum never let the Texas Ranger finish his warning. He judged distance and swung his Colt, connecting solidly with the base of the lawman's neck. The Ranger tumbled forward, unconscious. Slocum fetched more rope and tied up the Ranger.

The man had been right. Slocum *had* walked into a den of rattlers. Captain Baylor not only took bribes, but he had also been in cahoots with Hale's rustling. When Hale had kidnapped Consuela, Baylor had provided a hiding place.

Slocum took on not only the Manning brothers' henchmen, but the entire squad of Texas Rangers as well.

It mattered little to him. One or a hundred, he would get Consuela away from them.

Slocum backtracked the two Rangers' trail until he found where they had ridden out from. A half-dozen small houses dotted a grassy, lush hollow in the middle of the sandy terrain. He guessed that a small well gave the water needed to turn this arid land green. Slocum settled down just over the crest of a sand dune and watched the comings and goings at the main ranch house.

By his count, there were three Rangers in addition to Captain Baylor in the main house. Two others, probably Peveler and Stevenson, had their horses in a corral and worked on grooming and feeding them. Slocum squinted into the setting sun. He didn't know how much time he had before the two Rangers he had waylaid got free of their ropes and came screaming to their commander. He might have killed them, but Slocum didn't have the stomach for gunning down helpless men, even if they were rustlers— and worse.

He would leave such things to men like Johnny Hale and Captain Baylor. There wasn't a thing in the world wrong with shooting a man who deserved it, but if the man wasn't shooting back, Slocum found other ways of stopping him.

Slocum came to his feet when two Rangers came from the main house and beckoned to Peveler and Stevenson. The four men got their horses saddled and rode out, going south. Slocum watched until they vanished. The only thing in that direction, as far as he knew, was the Rio Grande. These four might be on their way to rustle some more Mexican beeves.

He hoped so. Ynocente Ochoa wouldn't mind parting with a few head of cattle in return for getting Consuela back. Those four leaving meant that Baylor and one other Ranger remained in the ranch house.

The odds had suddenly got much better. He only hoped that Consuela Suarez was being held here. If they had her somewhere else, or if they had killed her, he was working in vain.

The sun dipped below the purple-and-dust-hazed Franklin Mountains, spreading a fan of golden light tinged with orange and blue throughout the sky. In another ten minutes twilight stalked the desert and a cold wind began blowing.

Slocum turned up his collar and mounted. It was time for him to get into action.

"Just hold on for a while longer, Consuela," he said under his breath. "You're going home real soon now."

He started down the slope leading to the main house.

16

The wind had changed suddenly from hot to cold when the sun went down. Slocum rode to the house from downwind, listening hard for any sound that might indicate he had been detected. He heard nothing, but the fragrant scent of stew made his nose twitch and his mouth water. He had a hard time remembering when his last meal had been.

He dismounted and tethered his horse behind the corral where the Rangers and the two cowboys had penned their animals. His horse nickered softly. He patted the black stallion's neck, making soothing noises until the horse quieted. Amid the sounds of other horses, Slocum didn't think this would draw any attention.

He waited almost ten minutes. The sound of forks and knives against tin plates echoed inside the ranch house. Those inside ate their stew and didn't give a thought in the world to anyone sneaking up on them.

Slocum circled around, making sure that he hadn't missed anything. The last thing he wanted to do was to walk into the ranch house and not know where the occupants were—or if he had miscounted.

He peered in a window. Shoveling food into their mouths were Captain Baylor and one other Ranger. Slocum waited several more minutes to see if anyone else appeared. No one did, and he began to get worried. Where was Consuela?

He had no real proof that Baylor was involved with Hale and the Mannings. Everything was just guesswork. The Texas Ranger captain might not be a rustler, yet he definitely knew Peveler and Stevenson had been here. The Rangers riding off with them hadn't taken them into custody. They had ridden off as equals.

Still—and the thought kept worrying away at Slocum —the two cowboys had been cleared of all murder charges. Judge Buckler might have been paid off, but he was a legal judge and the "not guilty" verdict carried the full force of the law in El Paso.

Slocum pushed that injustice from his mind. He couldn't be wrong about Captain Baylor being tied in with Hale and his rustlers. That had to be the simple truth. Did the Ranger captain know anything about Consuela, though?

That worried Slocum most. Don Ynocente wasn't blowing smoke when he said he and his brother would lead a full-sized army into El Paso and take the town apart. He meant it when he said that Consuela had to be rescued by noon.

"Should I take a plate of this in to her?" the Ranger asked.

"Let her starve. She tried to bite me when I fed her breakfast," said Captain Baylor.

Slocum let out a huge lungful of breath he hadn't even known he was holding. Consuela *was* their prisoner!

"She's a feisty one, I'll give her that," the Ranger said.

"What we're going to do with her is a poser, though," said Baylor. "I wish to hell that Hale had the sense God gave a mule. Grabbing her only stirred up Ochoa."

"So raiding his rancho and taking his horses wouldn't?" asked the other.

"Ochoa would put up with anything except grabbing her."

"I reckon so, Captain. Maybe we can ransom her back. Ochoa would pay a king's ransom for her."

Slocum frowned as he puzzled over the men's words. They talked as if Ynocente would do anything to get Consuela back—as if she were *his* daughter rather than the daughter of his foreman. Don Ynocente had seemed more than decently protective of the girl, and Slocum couldn't figure out why. The Mexican rancher would do much for a mistress, but would be start a border war?

"I don't want him knowing we had anything to do with it. Damn that Hale! Why'd he have to go and get himself killed by Stoudenmirer?"

"Always was an idiot," said the Ranger. The man picked his teeth with a long, slender-bladed knife, then asked, "How much longer you going to put up with his two henchmen?"

"They still serve their purpose. If Ochoa catches them, we can still blame Hale or his men for the rustling."

"He wouldn't be none too gentle with them, not with him suspecting them of kidnapping her." The Ranger gestured with his knife toward a barred door at the rear of the main room.

Slocum didn't wait to hear Captain Baylor's answer. He slipped through the dusk as quietly as a shadow crossing a shadow. He tried to find a window to the room the Ranger had indicated and failed. Seeing a few boxes and a rain barrel, he decided to try exploring higher ground. Slocum dragged the boxes into a heap and climbed up, taking pains to move quietly. Having the Rangers come boiling out of the house, six-guns blazing, wasn't to his liking.

On the flat roof he moved carefully, testing the purchase with each step to make sure weakened timbers didn't sag and give him away. He found a spot in the roof directly over the room the Ranger had indicated—or so Slocum hoped. He pulled out his knife from the sheath on his belt and carefully gouged away at the roofing material, getting dirt and tarpaper pulled away from a tiny opening. He dropped flat on the roof and stuck his eye against the hole.

Directly below, a small pile of debris had fallen—and

looking up at him, wondering what was happening, was Consuela Suarez!

He started to call out to her, then bit back his words. Any loud noise would be heard by Baylor and the other Ranger. Slocum worked his knife around in the hole until he widened it enough to get a good view of the room. Consuela was securely fastened with hemp rope to a heavy four-legged wooden chair. A gag had been thrust into her mouth and fastened into place with a leather thong. She strained against her bonds and threw her head from side to side. All she succeeded in doing was tiring herself.

Slocum tried to see anything else in the room that might aid her escape. Except for the chair and a low three-legged stool, the room was empty. He cut a hole large enough to stick his hand through. He fumbled around trying to determine how secure the roof was.

"Damn," he muttered to himself. More than a knife was needed to cut through the thick wood he found. Slocum had been lucky finding this weak spot. As far as he could reach through the hole, he felt only heavy wood planking. Consuela was as secure in the windowless room as if she had been locked up in the El Paso town jail.

Some other way had to be found to get her free.

The door to the small room was flung open unexpectedly. Slocum had been so busy worrying at the hole in the roof, trying to enlarge it, that he hadn't been paying any attention to the Rangers' movements in the main room.

Standing silhouetted by light from the fireplace in the main room was Captain Baylor.

"You want some dinner? You're gonna have to behave yourself." He laughed when Consuela tried futilely to kick him. Her ankles had been secured to the chair legs. All she did was throw herself over onto her side.

Slocum cursed when he saw the Texas Ranger captain move to pick the woman up and set her chair on its legs again. Baylor froze. Slocum reached for his pistol and tried to get the muzzle back through the hole before Captain Baylor left the room.

He was too late by seconds.

Baylor had seen the debris that had fallen from the ceiling. A single look upward and Slocum's mission was no longer secret.

Slocum threw caution to the winds. He pulled his Colt out of the tiny hole, rolled onto his back, and came to his feet. He tried to figure where the two men below would poke their heads up when they came for him. Too much space prevented him from following that lead. He couldn't defend; he had to attack.

Slocum jumped off the roof and landed hard at the back of the ranch house. He dashed to the south wall and peered around, ready to shoot if he saw either man. Nothing. He scowled. This seemed too easy. He advanced more cautiously, thinking they might be waiting for him at the front of the house.

He spun around, Colt cocked and ready for a fight. The tension he felt turned into curiosity. Neither had emerged from the house—or had they?

If Baylor and his partner had both gone in the opposite direction looking for him, thinking there was safety in numbers, that left Consuela unguarded.

Slocum peered into the main room of the ranch house. Empty. He saw his chance and took it. Using his knife, he pried open the small window sash and wriggled inside. His Colt wandered in a slow arc, ready for action. No one remained in the room.

The door to the storeroom where Consuela was a prisoner had been barred on the outside once more. Slocum pulled off the heavy plank and tossed it aside. He threw open the door, pistol leveled and ready, in case Baylor had baited a trap and was ready to ambush him.

Consuela struggled against her bonds, muttering through the gag in her mouth. Slocum once more checked the outer room, then took two quick steps to Consuela's side and used the knife to sever the ropes. They parted with a soft sigh. The woman ripped the gag from her mouth, panting harshly.

"Oh, John, I thought you would never find me!"

"Where did they go?"

She kicked free of the ropes around her ankles and put her arms around him. She tried to kiss him but he pushed her back.

"Where did they go?" he repeated harshly. "We're not out of this yet."

"I do not know. Baylor saw the dust on the floor, then looked up and saw you through the hole. He ran from the room, barring the door after him. What they did after that, I cannot say." She clung to him. He almost dragged her from the storeroom.

"Please, John. My legs. I cannot walk."

"You're going to have to or we're both dead," he said harshly. Whatever Baylor had in mind, it smelled like a trap to Slocum. When would it get sprung? He knew he would find out all too soon.

"There is no way out other than the door," Consuela said. "I escaped from them for a moment, and ran about looking. That is it."

"Back to the window." He shoved her in the direction of the window he had entered through. Slocum bobbed his head out and back as fast as he could, but it almost wasn't fast enough. One of the Rangers opened fire the instant his Stetson passed through the window.

"Another hole in it," he said wearily. "I'm going to charge Ynocente for a new hat."

"What are we to do?" Consuela asked. He looked at her. In spite of her captivity, she looked fit, and heart-stoppingly beautiful. Her dark hair spun about her head in wild disarray, floating like a black and lustrous mist. She wore a cowboy's clothing, and it flapped about her trim body like the canvas sails of a windjammer.

Slocum smiled. "The last time I saw you, you were buck naked." He laughed when she blushed.

"They gave me clothes when we arrived at this place. We are in Texas, no?"

"We are in Texas, yes," he answered. "About five miles outside the eastern side of El Paso."

"If we get horses, we can be across the Rio Grande in an hour."

She made it sound so easy. Slocum slowly opened the window; a bullet smashed the glass. The Ranger hadn't budged an inch.

"They'll have the front door covered, too. The window and the door are the only ways out—or in." His green eyes went to the ceiling. He had feared walking on the roof might reveal a weak spot and send him crashing down. From this side he saw that the roof had been solidly constructed. Too solidly, for his taste.

"Put out the cooking fire."

"But why? You would burn this place to the ground with us in it?"

"That's a powerful big fireplace."

"John, no!" Consuela exclaimed.

"Afraid of getting your fancy new duds dirty?" he chided. Slocum went to the front door while Consuela worked to pull the smoldering cooking fire logs from the fireplace. He saw a shape move; he fired. Captain Baylor shouted angrily at him.

"It is done. But . . ."

"Do it. Shinny on up," he told her.

"It is very cramped. I can make it, I think, but your shoulders might be too wide."

"If you get to the roof and I can't, I'll draw their fire. My horse is tethered on the other side of the corral to the south. Get on the horse and ride for home. You can make it in a couple of hours. The stallion is strong. Don't worry about tiring him out none."

"John, I will not leave you like this!"

"Get on up. I might be able to fit." He swatted her on the rump to get her moving. Consuela glowered at him, then turned and flung her arms around his neck and kissed him full on the lips. She parted regretfully. Her voice was a low, husky whisper. "That is only part of what I owe you, *querido.*"

With that, Consuela kicked through the ashes and began working her way up the chimney. Slocum went to the window and fired twice at the Ranger posted there. He rushed back to the front door in time to take a potshot at Baylor as he tried to rush in.

"Just wait 'em out," Baylor called, "just like we planned."

Slocum had to admit that the trap had worked well. Although he moved about freely inside the ranch house, it was only a bigger prison cell than the storeroom where they had kept Consuela. Sooner or later, he would slip up and they would have him.

If the two Texas Rangers got tired of waiting, they could burn the house down around his ears.

A cascade of soot filled the room. Consuela had reached the roof. Slocum hurried to the fireplace and looked up the narrow chimney. He didn't know if he would make it, but there was no other way. He saw Consuela's silhouette above him on the roof, her soft words urging him to hurry. Slocum squeezed his shoulders together until pain shot up his back. Then he began climbing.

Scooting painfully, scraping skin off his back, he made slow progress upward—but he fit!

He gasped in relief when his shoulders popped free of the chimney top. From below he heard boots pounding on the ranch house floor. He tried to get free of the chimney before they figured out where he and Consuela had gone.

Slocum almost made it. He heard Captain Baylor swear and then hot lead tore along the back of his right leg. The burning pain convinced him to move faster. He spilled onto the roof, blood oozing from the narrow wound that started on his left calf and went up to his buttocks. The bullet had lodged in a fleshy part that would make riding a tad on the painful side, but he was willing to try.

"Come on," he cried, tugging on Consuela's hand. He got to the front of the house and looked over in time to see the Ranger lifting his pistol. Slocum fired twice, both bullets finding their target. The Ranger crumpled to the ground like a discarded piece of foolscap. He didn't even stir.

"Come on out, Baylor," he called. "I got you where you had me."

Even as he spoke, he motioned for Consuela to drop over the roof's edge. He *didn't* have the Ranger captain trapped, and it wouldn't take Baylor long to figure that out. Slocum couldn't possibly watch both window and door at the same time.

Slocum waited until Consuela motioned that she had found his stallion. Only then did Slocum drop over the verge. He cried out in pain as his injured leg buckled under him.

This erratic movement caused by his game leg saved his life. Baylor had come to the door and fired at the sound of Slocum hitting the ground. Slocum fired twice, driving the Ranger captain back into the house.

"Hurry, John. Get on!"

Slocum's left leg was too weak to support him getting up into the saddle. He went around to the right side and jumped over, almost knocking Consuela out of the saddle.

They urged the powerful stallion into the night, heading due south. Behind came the sharp report from Captain Baylor's Colt, but the bullets missed by a mile.

"We got out just in time," Slocum said. "I'm out of ammunition." He held up his Colt Navy and pulled the trigger. The hammer fell on a spent chamber.

Consuela laughed, hiccoughed, then started to cry. She put her arms around his midsection and buried her face in his shoulder, her tears soaking into his sooty shirt. Slocum looked up and found the springtime constellations, got his bearings, and rode like all the demons of hell followed him.

He wasn't sure if the crooked Texas Ranger coming after him wasn't worse.

17

Slocum hadn't ridden a mile when he realized that they could never cross the Rio Grande in time. Captain Baylor would be on them like a swarm of bees going for a honeycomb. If he hadn't been wounded in the leg, Slocum thought they might be able to outride anyone, even with both of them on the strong stallion's back, but each step the horse took sent knives of pain into Slocum's body.

"You're weaving around, John. Are you all right?"

"Getting giddy. I haven't lost much blood, but the pain is almost more than I can stand. Can't figure it. Been wounded worse than this and it never affected me like this."

Consuela yelped and tightened her hold around his waist. This was all that kept Slocum from tumbling off.

"We must tend your wound."

"No, wait," he said. "Not here. We've got to ride for a while longer." He studied the spring stars and found the handle of the Little Dipper and the North Star. Slocum pulled his horse around and went due east.

"Where do we go?" Consuela demanded. "Mexico is not in this direction."

"Hueco Tanks is, though. We can get lost in the rocks, find water, hole up for a spell. Baylor might not expect us to go this way. Tracking in the dark isn't possible, especially now that the wind is kicking up the sand."

Clouds of dust whipped along the ridges of the desolate dunes. The same wind that occasionally blinded him also erased their tracks. If Captain Baylor failed to see them, he could never track them down. All Slocum had to do was outwit the Texas Ranger.

All he had to do . . .

The next hour Slocum alternately drifted off and jerked awake as pain shot up his leg and into his body.

"When do we stop?" asked Consuela. Slocum wasn't sure if she wanted to stop because she was tired or out of concern for him. It didn't matter. Slocum had reached the end of his endurance.

"Here. This looks like a decent spot. We can see anyone coming and still stay hidden." The pile of rocks provided a good campsite, too. Boulders would shield them from the wind and hide a cookfire from prying eyes.

Consuela lithely jumped from behind. She almost fell when Slocum dismounted and found that his left leg refused to support his weight. Consuela's arms wrapped around him and helped him to the ground.

"Feels better just being out of the saddle." Slocum winced as he stretched his left leg straight. He rolled onto his right side to alleviate the pain. It didn't work.

Consuela went about setting up camp. Slocum used his knife to split his denims up the back of the leg and reveal the extent of the bullet wound. The lead had gouged out a shallow channel along his calf and the upper part of his thigh before embedding in his ass. He hadn't been seriously hurt, but it sent jolts of pain through him that made him grind his teeth.

"There," Consuela said. "All is ready for some dinner. You have very little in your saddlebags to eat, though."

"I hadn't planned to make an expedition of rescuing you," he said.

"Let me look at your wound." Consuela giggled like a young girl when she saw the nature of his injury.

"You're going to have to dig out the bullet. You ever done anything like this before?"

"No," she said.

Slocum heaved a sigh. "That means I may never be able to ride again."

"I have taken out bullets before. Never one in such a place." Again she giggled. "I am boiling water. Let me get some."

Slocum gritted his teeth when Consuela poured some of the boiling water onto his blood-oozing leg. She worked upward, tending to each part of the wound until she came to the bullet itself.

"I will have to take off your trousers." Slocum wriggled and grunted until he was free of them. He had alternate chills and fever from the warm fire and cold wind, the feel of Consuela's cool hands on his flesh and the burning bullet in his butt.

He stiffened as he felt the tip of the knife against his rear end, then nothing.

"There," Consuela said, holding out the bullet. "Do you want this as a souvenir?"

"Throw it away," he said. "If I saved every damn bullet that's been taken out of me, I'd be carrying saddlebags weighing a ton."

"You exaggerate," she said, her fingers working over his legs. "Not by much, though. You have many scars."

Slocum relaxed, feeling better than he had in hours.

"You need further attention to the wound," Consuela said.

"With the bullet out, there won't be any blood poisoning," he said. "Unless you can stitch up the hole, there's not much else you can do for me."

"No, John, there is more. Let me kiss it and make it well." Consuela slipped down and Slocum felt her hot breath against his skin. Her soft lips kissed here and there. In spite of the tiredness that had slowly washed over Slocum like a gentle ocean wave, he found himself becoming aroused. Consuela carefully rolled him onto his back. He never noticed the brief jab of pain. Her lips made sure of that by moving softly, wetly, arousingly over his groin.

"I said I owed you much, John. Let me try to repay it now."

"Only a bit, Consuela," he said, his hands stroking through her long raven's-wing dark hair. Slocum lay back and let her minister to him. He felt his fleshy spike hardening as she kissed and licked and stroked her fingers over him.

"Only a bit?" she mocked, lifting her face and staring at him.

"I lied. I want a lot. I want it all!"

She moved up his body like a snake slithering up a tree. As if by magic, she shucked out of the too-large jeans she wore. The plaid shirt popped open and revealed her firm, high breasts. Slocum reached up and took those ripe melons and began rotating them slowly, his thumbs and forefingers squeezing down on the nipples. He felt the hard buttons begin to pulse faster as the woman's heart raced.

Consuela swung her bare leg over his waist and settled down, their crotches grinding together. Slocum moaned when Consuela reached between them and captured his harness and guided it toward her yielding, softly opening nether lips. Slocum felt warmth and moistness surround him as Consuela sank down fully. Her fleshy rump rose into the air as she bent forward to kiss him.

"This is the best reward I ever got," he told her.

Ruby lips closed on his. They kissed, their passion mounting by the second. Consuela's full lips parted and her pink tongue darted forth to engage Slocum's. They played a game of oral hide-and-seek, hinting at more erotic pleasures that would happen very soon.

"Umm, no, do not take your hands from my breasts. They feel so good there. As if they belong there!"

Consuela shoved her chest down into Slocum's cupped

hands and began rotating her body slightly so that her nipples dragged over his callused palms. Slocum kept his left hand on her breast but moved his right down her slightly domed belly and lower.

His fingers tangled in the soft fleece he found. He touched all the right spots. Consuela gasped in passion, then began moving her hips in a circular motion that built both their desires to the breaking point.

"This is so good, John. I could stay like this forever."

"I can't. You're so tight around me. Faster. Do more. I can't move like this."

She had him pinned to the ground, but he did not mind. Not at all. He was coming totally alive as she moved above him. When Consuela pulled her hips up and let him almost slip out, Slocum started to protest. Consuela gave him no time. Her hips came ramming back like a runaway locomotive. She slammed wetly into him and squeezed with her inner muscles.

His hands roved up and down the woman's arched back, tracing out every bone in her spine. Slocum lifted himself up slightly to find her lips. They kissed deeply as Consuela continued to slide up and down, impaled on Slocum's thick length.

Slocum cupped her tight buttocks and began squeezing and kneading, as if he had trapped two fleshy gobs of dough. Consuela's gasps and moans became incoherent as lust mounted. Slocum gripped firmly and guided her in the rhythm he found most exciting.

"Can't take much more," he told her as he nibbled at her tender ear. Slocum gripped tighter on her fleshy asscheeks when his balls tightened. He felt as if she was going to rip him out by the roots—and he wanted more!

Consuela pumped furiously now, her body slamming repeatedly into his. Her breasts jiggled and bounced. Her face took on a mask of pure carnal craving as orgasm seized her.

Slocum tried to hang on. He couldn't. The crushing tightness around him, the motion of Consuela's body above him, the sweat-slippery feel of her buttocks all drove him over the edge of desire. He exploded, spewing his seed into her yearning cavity.

Spent, Slocum slumped back. All the energy he had felt during their lovemaking now vanished and betrayed how exhausted he was. Consuela straightened her legs and lay fully atop him, her breasts crushed on his chest.

"It is always so good with you, John," she said.

He couldn't argue, but other thoughts disturbed him. "What would your father say if he knew?"

"He would not be pleased. He wants me to marry Don Juan's eldest son."

Slocum frowned. "What does Don Ynocente say to this?"

"He has consented. I believe the idea came from him, though this has never been said."

Slocum had thought that Ynocente and Consuela might be sneaking off together and that she was his mistress, but this revelation meant that Ynocente wanted to combine his ranch with his brother's through the marriage. It had seemed strange that Ynocente thought of his foreman's daughter as if she were his own. What a dowry his entire spread would make!

"Does Don Juan's son know you aren't a virgin?"

"No."

"Does Ynocente?"

"Why do you care, John? I know my own mind. Those rules are made to keep women in their place. I do what I like."

"What does Ynocente think happened between you and Luke Manning?"

"You ask too many questions. That means you do not have enough to occupy your mind—and other things."

Consuela began wriggling against him. Slocum had

thought he was too tired to respond. He was wrong. She coaxed a new erection. This time he rolled on top of her and found that the bullet wound didn't bother some things at all.

But for the pleasure he received, he would have endured a considerable amount of hurt.

Slocum awoke an hour before dawn, his arms around Consuela. The darkness seemed absolute and the hard points of the stars so sharp that he wondered if he could cut himself on them. He had tried not to stir too much but his tiny movement woke Consuela.

"Are we going now?" she asked sleepily.

"We'd better. Ynocente is going to burn El Paso to the ground by noon if you're not back."

She did not respond. She snuggled closer, her face buried in the hollow of his shoulder. Finally, Consuela said in a soft voice, "Do I have to return?"

"Of course."

"I do not want to. I want to stay with you, John. There is nothing for me across the river. With you, there is everything!"

"I'd call it just the other way around," Slocum said. "You're engaged to Don Juan's son. The Ochoa family is rich and powerful. Me, I got enough money in my jeans to get me to Tucson or Lamy or maybe Amarillo, if I head that way."

"I have never seen these places."

"They're nothing to brag on," said Slocum.

"It would not matter, as long as we are together."

She kissed his shoulder and moved to his neck and ear. Slocum lay staring at the dark sky, sharing some of that blackness with his soul. He and Ynocente went back a long ways. They had proven their friendship in blood. And Slocum was actually considering running off with Consuela and to hell with Ynocente.

What should it matter to the don? Consuela wasn't his flesh and blood. Sure, he had pledged her to marry his nephew, but Slocum going off with Consuela was an affront to his brother, not directly to Ynocente. Juan and Slocum shared much the same past as he and Ynocente did, but they had never been as close.

"He'd never stop looking for me. There's something in Ynocente that makes you special to him."

"Special? Pah!"

Even as she denied it, Slocum knew Consuela had wondered about her unique treatment by Ynocente Ochoa, too. The daughter of a valued foreman might receive education and special privileges, but not the full attention of the powerful *patrón* himself. Slocum had thought Consuela was Ynocente's mistress, but now he dismissed that idea completely.

"Would you want a man who lied and broke his word?" Slocum asked.

"What? You are not like that, John. You are the most honorable man I have ever met!"

"Honor is about all that's left to me."

"We can be together!"

Slocum had promised Ynocente to return the kidnapped girl. Friendship dictated that he do so. When he had gone after her, he had intended to do so. What did he really feel for Consuela? Was it love? Was this love strong enough to blot out his honor-bound duty?

He kissed her squarely on her lush, full lips, then pushed her away, saying, "We can cross the Rio Grande before sunup and be at the hacienda before noon."

Consuela's face flowed from stunned disbelief to fierce anger. She spun away from him and dressed in stony silence. Slocum didn't blame her. He wasn't certain that he wasn't making the worst mistake of his life. And for what? A misguided sense of duty? Honor?

He shook himself, stretched mightily, and sat up, the

morning stillness settling around him like a cool blanket. Doing the honorable thing was never wrong.

He dressed and started breaking camp. Neither of them mentioned breakfast—or felt much like eating.

13

Slocum gave up trying to talk sense to Consuela. She rode behind him in stony silence. He felt the tenseness of her body every time the horse turned. She normally rode expertly, flowing with the lines of the stallion. Now she swung to and fro as if she were made of unyielding wood.

By the time pink fingers of dawn streaked the sky, they had reached the Rio Grande. Slocum's every sense strained for any hint of pursuit. Captain Baylor didn't have many men he could call on to hunt them down. Slocum hoped that by going east and resting, he had thrown the Texas Ranger off his trail. Patrolling the river, even with a full squad of men, was not an easy task.

"Is there any better place to ford?" Slocum asked Consuela. She said nothing. If he hadn't heard the grinding of her teeth, he might have thought she had died.

He studied the once raging, spring-runoff-engorged river. It had narrowed to a muddy band half its former glory. Crossing would be much easier, especially if he found a shallow spot. In another week the mighty Rio Grande would be a damp memory.

Slocum got across with a minimum of trouble, even without Consuela's help. The ride to the Ochoa hacienda felt like he was riding to his own execution. All Consuela had to do was tell Ynocente what had happened the night before—and just before Hale's raid on the hacienda and immediately after Slocum had rescued her from Luke Manning. Any of those indiscretions would ignite a blood feud. Slocum hadn't forced the fiery Latin beauty. Quite the contrary. Consuela had relished every instant of their lovemaking.

Ynocente Ochoa would not see it that way. Friendship meant nothing when honor was betrayed. Unmarried women did not do what Consuela had done without being called whores. Ynocente could never call her that, therefore Slocum had forced himself on her and disgraced the Ochoa name. That was the way Ynocente would see it.

"Are you going to tell Don Ynocente about us?" asked Slocum.

Consuela said nothing.

"He'll kill me—or try. I'm not sure that he can. I wouldn't want to hurt him, but if it comes down to him or me, I'd as soon drop you off here and let you walk the rest of the way. Ynocente is a friend and I don't like killing friends."

"I should tell him."

Slocum reined in. "Off."

"But I will not," Consuela went on, her tone sullen. "We are meant for one another, you and I. How can you deny me?"

"I've been asking myself that," said Slocum. "In my own way, honor means as much to me as it does to Ynocente."

"Pah! Men. You know nothing of honor, yet you prattle on about it endlessly." She seemed to relax, her arms snaking around his waist and hands clasping in front. She leaned her head against his back. "I will not tell him. I would not want to see either of you killed, and you are right. One would die."

"Maybe both. I could shoot Ynocente, but your father commands a rancho full of vaqueros."

"My father." Consuela said it as if doubting her parentage. "He is a good man, but weak."

"I don't see him that way," said Slocum, remembering how Pedro Suarez had shown his bravery any number of times. It had taken courage to charge Johnny Hale's position down by the Rio Grande.

"Men." With that Consuela fell silent again.

Slocum rode another thirty minutes before coming to the elaborate wrought-iron gate marking the entrance to the Ochoa hacienda. He knew that word of their arrival had already been relayed ahead. Many field hands had seen him and Consuela riding along. One vaquero carrying the message would have been enough. He counted no fewer than ten working the herds. Don Ynocente's ear might be deaf from listening to all the reports.

Slocum reined in and helped Consuela down. Ynocente, Pedro Suarez, and Consuela's *dueña* awaited them just inside the dark passageway leading to the inner courtyard. Slocum dismounted and handed the reins to a stableboy.

"Grain," he ordered for his steed. "He's worked hard carrying double weight, and he deserves a reward." The boy's head bobbed up and down as he led the big horse away.

Slocum turned to face Ynocente.

"You have returned with her. *Bueno*. I do not need to order the army across to burn El Paso to the ground."

"She's back," Slocum said, hollow inside. He had made a lot of mistakes in his day. He wondered if returning with Consuela instead of taking her suggestion and riding off together wasn't another blunder, and bigger than most. "She can marry Don Juan's son now."

"She told you, eh? She is a good girl."

"Captain Baylor had her," Slocum said bluntly. "Baylor is behind most of the trouble along the river. He and Hale were in chaoots doing the rustling."

"But Hale worked for the Mannings."

"Some men have two masters. I'm not even sure the Manning brothers knew about Hale and Baylor. They may have. It doesn't matter. Hale's dead. You have Consuela back."

"Thank you, my friend. This is a debt that can never be repaid."

"Just keep an eye peeled for Captain Baylor. He's the enemy, not anyone in El Paso."

"Frank and Doc Manning can never be friends."

Slocum shrugged. "No need to be friends. Just don't start shooting at each other when you see one another. That might be good enough until you can come to a more permanent truce."

"Baylor must pay for what he has done."

Slocum shook his head. That would only mean more bloodshed along the border, yet he knew that honor demanded it. Ynocente felt violated. Slocum wasn't sure that he didn't agree. Letting the crooked Ranger get by with kidnapping and rustling and murder rankled.

"See Marshal Stoudenmirer. I don't think he has any love for Baylor." Slocum heard the pounding of hooves on the road leading to the hacienda. He turned to see a vaquero dive from his still running horse and stagger. He came to a halt in front of Ynocente. The vaquero spoke in Spanish too rapid for Slocum to follow. He caught the El Paso marshal's name several times but couldn't even get the drift of the message.

"Speak of the Devil and he appears," said Ynocente. "My vaquero has come from the border. Your Marshal Stoudenmirer desires a peace talk with Don Juan and me. He wants me to—how do you say it—swear out an arrest warrant for Peveler and Stevenson for kidnapping."

Slocum smiled at this. Stoudenmirer moved in strange ways, but he got the job done. Arresting Hale's men again put more pressure on Captain Baylor. If either cowboy spilled his guts to keep from being sent to the Federal Penitentiary in Detroit, Baylor's neck was shoved into a noose. When Dallas Stoudenmirer broke the power of the Texas Rangers, he would be the undisputed authority in the area.

Power, Slocum thought. Power was at the bottom of it all, and Stoudenmirer worked well to get it.

"Will you come with me, John?" asked Ynocente. "I do not trust this Stoudenmirer as you do."

"Can't say I trust the son of a bitch," admitted Slocum, "but I surely do admire the way he gets things done."

"Then you will come. Fetch your horse. We ride immediately."

Slocum started to protest. He had been through hell getting Consuela back, and in spite of the night's rest, interrupted by the bouts of passionate lovemaking, he still needed sleep. His wound throbbed but the pain had tapered off to the point where it was bearable.

"Let's get this over," he said. The stableboy returned quickly with his stallion. The horse seemed in better shape than its rider.

Ynocente, Pedro, Slocum and a half-dozen well-armed vaqueros rode directly to the Rio Grande, crossing within two hours and arriving in the center of El Paso in another hour. Dallas Stoudenmirer leaned against the wall of the Ben Dowell Saloon, his gold badge shining in the bright noonday sun.

"Howdy, gents," the marshal said. "Glad y'all decided to take my offer of a truce. There's been enough bad blood on both sides of the Rio Grande."

"There is much to discuss," said Ynocente Ochoa. The *patrón* and the marshal went into the saloon. Slocum, Pedro, and the others stayed outside, alert for any trouble. Slocum saw Frank Manning at the far end of the street, but the man didn't try to enter his own saloon. Stoudenmirer had laid claim to it and all Manning could do was collect the profits. An hour after Stoudenmirer and Ochoa had entered, they came out together.

Slocum saw that all had gone well. Ochoa smiled, something he had not done in quite a while.

"We got it all worked out, Slocum," said the marshal. "A few of us are going to ride on out to the Marsh Ranch and arrest Peveler and Stevenson for kidnapping Consuela Suarez. If we get lucky, we might even find evidence of new cattle rustling."

"What about Captain Baylor?" Slocum asked.

"He's a captain in the Texas Rangers. Can't do much about him on hearsay, now can I?"

"I reckon you want me to go along," Slocum said, knowing the answer before he saw Ynocente's curt nod.

"You might prove useful since it was you who got the girl free of their clutches."

Slocum saw how Stoudenmirer skirted the real issue of a Ranger being involved in crimes against damned near everyone on both sides of the border. With Hale's two cowboys taking the blame, the Rangers couldn't get too riled, and Baylor would know he was being watched.

Slocum saw that and he suspected the marshal of plotting even more. Stoudenmirer had worked methodically and well to rid the El Paso area of owlhoots. Slocum didn't figure he would stop until Baylor was behind bars or dead.

The ride to the Marsh Ranch went quicker than it had the night before. They had no reason to conceal their approach. At the gate, Slocum pointed. "Over that hill lies the ranch house."

"Been here once or twice on law business," said Stoudenmirer, working to get the tips of his mustache into sharp points. "If I was Peveler and Stevenson, I'd hightail it due south toward Mexico when we come charging up to the front door." Stoudenmirer motioned. All his deputies left to ride in a wide circle that Slocum knew would end up between the ranch house and the border to cut off escape.

"They might try to go east into the Hueco Mountains, too," Slocum said.

"Reckon so," admitted Stoudenmirer. "If a few vaqueros went in that direction, they might be able to knock a fleeing fugitive out of the saddle with a single rifle shot."

Ynocente spoke rapidly in Spanish and dispatched four of his men. The remaining three hung back as Slocum,

Stoudenmirer, and Ynocente Ochoa walked their horses up the road to the ranch house.

"This might be risky," said Stoudenmirer. "You two just remember you ain't deputies. You're just law-abidin' citizens out for an afternoon of pleasurable riding."

"They kidnapped Consuela," Ynocente said coldly.

"The courts will convict them, then," said Stoudenmirer.

The marshal checked his leather-lined left pocket and the long-barreled Colt dangling butt-forward at his right hip. Only then did he spur his horse on and around the bend in the road to the ranch house.

Slocum saw that they were in luck. The horses in the corral showed that no fewer than five men had returned.

"Howdy, Ranger," Stoudenmirer said to a lawman who looked up from his work near the corral. "We got warrants for Chris Peveler and Frank Stevenson. You happen to know where they are?"

"Inside with Captain Baylor."

"You wouldn't want to go and obstruct justice, would you, Ranger?" Stoudenmirer asked in a voice with a steel edge.

"I'm a lawman, too, Marshal."

"Then just let me and your captain work this out ourselves. Why not take your friend over there in the barn— the one with the rifle trained on us—with you? I'm sure that some . . . rustlers might be prowling around. Go check on them."

Slocum appreciated how Stoudenmirer got rid of Captain Baylor's support, giving them a way out with just a hint of threat to it. The two Rangers saddled their horses and rode out, never looking back. Slocum wasn't sure if either would be seen in these parts again. Rangers' stars, like a tattered suit of clothes, could be discarded easily enough, given the right motivation.

"Two down, three to go."

"The dangerous three," said Slocum.

"Let us not waste time talking about it," said Ynocente. He pulled a carbine with worn stocks from his saddle sheath and levered a shell into the chamber.

"Arrest first, shoot later—if necessary." Stoudenmirer climbed from his horse and put his hand in his coat pocket. He was ready for a fight, and so was John Slocum.

Slocum had been kicked around enough. It was time to settle scores.

Someone inside saw them before they got to the door. A loud shout and a bullet came simultaneously. Ynocente returned fire and all hell broke loose.

Slocum dived for cover at the same instant he remembered the solitary window on the side of the building. He rolled and came to his feet, but his wounded left leg betrayed him. He couldn't support his own weight and he collapsed, wincing in agony. Slocum started crawling, but by the time he reached the side, he saw a broad back vanishing around the house. One of the men inside had escaped.

Slocum got his feet under him to cut off further escape. He rose up in front of the window, Colt ready. He shoved the barrel into the face of Frank Stevenson as the man tried to climb through.

"Hold it!" shouted Slocum.

Stevenson threw himself to one side, banging hard against the window frame. Slocum fired, the bullet sailing past his intended target and into the main room of the house. Frank Stevenson started firing wildly, forcing Slocum back. He saw an exposed arm and fired. Stevenson yowled in pain. Slocum took no delight from wounding the man. He wanted to do more.

Slocum fired twice more, then got his chance. He heard Stevenson backing from the window. Slocum's legs bent under him like springs. He hurled himself through the window, landing hard on his belly. Stevenson nursed his injured arm. Slocum's gun leveled.

A blast of pain lanced through Slocum's chest as Baylor kicked him hard in the ribs.

The world turned red around him as he fought to keep from passing out. Slocum heard gunshots. He tried to decide where he'd been shot. The only pain in his body came from old injuries. He struggled to his knees, Colt still clutched in his hand.

Dallas Stoudenmirer stood in the doorway of the house, smoking pistol in his hand. Frank Stevenson lay sprawled on his back. His eyes already glazed over with death.

"Got the son of a bitch."

"Baylor. Did you get Baylor?" Slocum gasped out the words. His ribs hurt too much to do more.

"Must have got out through the window when I came busting in."

"Damn." Slocum got to his feet, knocked out the spent brass from his six-shooter, and reloaded.

"John," called Ynocente. "Are you able to go after him?"

"Them," Slocum said grimly. "Both Peveler and Baylor got away."

"I will join you."

"You two go after Peveler, since you've got the warrant for him," said Slocum. The slow smile crossing Dallas Stoudenmirer's face told Slocum this was what the marshal wanted. If Slocum happened to kill the Ranger captain, fine. If the El Paso marshal—and ex-Texas Ranger—did the killing, there'd be political hell to pay for months.

They left Stevenson's cadaver on the floor and went outside. Slocum strained to hear receding hoofbeats. Captain Baylor was the last out. This had to be the Texas Ranger. Slocum swung into his saddle and grunted. The pain in his rear magnified with every movement. He hadn't suffered much from the captain kicking him in the ribs, but the wound the Ranger inflicted on him when he'd rescued Consuela burned like fire.

Slocum took off at a gallop after the fleeing Ranger. He

got to the top of a sand dune and looked over the ranch. The dust cloud heading toward the border betrayed Baylor. Slocum set off to catch him.

Through the afternoon, Slocum slowly closed the distance. When he came on Baylor's horse whinnying pitifully and thrashing about on the ground with a broken leg, Slocum knew he had the renegade Texas Ranger. Slocum dismounted and went to the horse. It had stepped in a prairie-dog hole. Slocum emotionlessly shot the horse just behind the ear to put it out of its misery.

"You're next, Baylor," called Slocum. The wind ate his words and muffled them in a small dust storm whipping across the desert.

Baylor had committed too many crimes hiding behind his badge. Rustling and murder and kidnapping were bad enough, but Slocum thought it was even worse that the man hadn't even had the decency to put his horse out of its misery. Some men weren't fit to live.

Slocum had to correct this injustice. He got back onto his stallion, pulled his hat lower on his forehead to protect his eyes from the blowing sand, and started off slowly. He figured Baylor would be lying in wait, ready to drygulch him.

But where? The dust storm was getting worse by the minute. Slocum didn't want to lose the Ranger now. This might be his only chance to settle the score.

Slocum's instincts saved him. The back of his neck began to prickle and the hair to rise. He threw himself forward and past his horse's head just as a bullet ripped through the air. If he had stayed upright in the saddle, he would have lost the top of his head.

His hat went fluttering off in the stiff breeze and Slocum tumbled to the ground. He lay still, waiting for Captain Baylor to come to him. Slocum didn't think the Ranger would make sure of his kill by putting another slug into his victim. Baylor needed Slocum's horse to get away, and a second shot might spook the spirited animal.

Slocum lay and waited for several minutes before he saw a figure moving through the brown curtain of dust, coming to be sure of his backshooting handiwork.

Slocum rolled and came to his knees, gun aimed at Baylor. "You've had this coming for quite a while, Cap'n," Slocum said. His finger tightened and the Colt bucked hard.

Baylor tried to respond. Slocum's bullet caught him square in the middle of the chest. He took half a step back and lost his balance. Arms outflung, he fell to the parched desert sand. Slocum got to his feet and went to the fallen lawman.

He bent over and ripped the star off Baylor's chest. "You don't deserve to wear this," Slocum said. There had never been any love lost between him and the Texas Rangers, but it galled him to see a blatantly crooked Ranger. "And you caused me one hell of a pain in the ass."

Slocum gingerly touched the spot where Captain Baylor had wounded him, then spun and walked away. Baylor didn't deserve a funeral. Let the buzzards and ants feast on his putrid flesh.

Slocum found his stallion, mounted, and rode past the fallen lawman without a backward glance.

19

Slocum wanted to get back across the border to Consuela, but Dallas Stoudenmirer and Ynocente Ochoa insisted that he have a victory drink at the Ben Dowell Saloon. Slocum thought he had been used enough by these two men. He had done Ynocente's dirty work, rescuing Consuela and bringing Hale and his men to bloody justice for murder, rustling, and their other crimes. These things he did not begrudge Ynocente for doing.

Stoudenmirer was another matter. The marshal had used him repeatedly to get back at the Mannings and the Texas Rangers. Slocum had eliminated the last trace of rivalry for power in El Paso when he had gunned down Captain Baylor. When that sorry story was made public, the Rangers would have a hard time recovering lost prestige and influence.

Through it all Dallas Stoudenmirer rode with clean hands and spotless reputation.

"Wanted to buy you a drink, Slocum. Least I can do considering your help in all this." Stoudenmirer motioned to Jake, who brought over a bottle. Stoudenmirer drank most of it while Slocum nursed his shot glass filled with the cheap whiskey.

"You making this your headquarters?" Slocum asked the marshal.

"Reckon so. A good place to watch what the Manning

boys are up to. Can't say I've broke their spirit, but getting rid of Johnny Hale is a start." Stoudenmirer smiled broadly, his thick mustache curling up at the ends as he did so. "They can't go running to that thievin' Ranger captain, either. I got 'em by the balls now. The whole damn town is mine!"

Slocum saw half a dozen men entering the saloon. He started to reach for his Colt when Ynocente stopped him. The man said softly, "Simply watch, John. There is nothing more to do but play the political games."

The portly man who led the small delegation cleared his throat. "Marshal Stoudenmirer, as alderman of El Paso, the people have entrusted me with showing you our gratitude for what you done in getting rid of Hale's rustlers and restoring peace along the border." The man nodded in Ynocente's direction. "We want to give you this token of our esteem for your fine work."

Another man passed over a gold-headed cane and presented it to Stoudenmirer.

Beaming, the marshal said, "I surely do deserve this, but it still pleases me that you've seen fit to honor me. Most towns just let their lawmen go unappreciated. This is the finest cane I've ever had the pleasure to see."

Stoudenmirer took the cane and twirled it in the air. The gold head gleamed and shone as it spun.

Slocum shook his head. Stoudenmirer had done damned little in ridding El Paso of the outlaws, but that didn't matter to the aldermen.

"Let the marshal have his moment in the sun," Ynocente. "We know who is responsible for the good things happening here."

"He's lapping it up like a hungry kitten going after milk," said Slocum. "Let's get back across the river."

"It is time," said Ynocente. "I have done my duty here as Juan's representative. Peace is guaranteed and all is well."

"No reason for any blood feud," agreed Slocum. "Not when those causing it are all dead."

They left the saloon and mounted. Slocum was glad to head south and cross the Rio Grande. Since they were alone, he wanted to say certain things to Ynocente on the ride, the rancher's vaqueros having ridden on ahead back to the hacienda. But Slocum didn't know how to go about telling Ynocente that he wanted Consuela to come with him when he rode on to Tucson.

Before he could get a handle on how to start, Ynocente spoke up. "There is a matter which must rest heavily on your mind. I wish to clear this up."

"What are you talking about?"

"My behavior where Consuela is concerned is not that of *patrón* to the young daughter of a trusted foreman. I am even marrying her off to Don Juan's eldest son, my rancho her dowry."

Slocum tensed. "Consuela had mentioned something of the sort."

"Such generosity is out of the ordinary, even for one as gracious as I." Ynocente chuckled, then sobered. "You may wonder why I do not have any children."

"The way you always tomcatted around, well, yeah, the thought has crossed my mind," Slocum admitted.

"Consuela is not my mistress, as you may have thought," Ynocente said. "She is my daughter."

Slocum blinked but kept his silence.

"When we were rustling cattle down in Laredo, I slept with Pedro's wife. A mortal sin, but she was very beautiful and I was unable to resist. Pedro does not know that Consuela is my daughter. His wife—such a lovely woman!—died giving birth to Consuela."

"You don't have any other children?"

"Not even any other bastards," Ynocente said sadly. "Soon after I lay with Consuela's mother, I left for the interior of Mexico. Do you remember?"

"You took off for about a month. I do remember. You were after Yaqui silver."

"I was after their silver; they were after me." Ynocente shrugged. "They caught a greedy and impetuous youth. They cut off his balls."

Slocum was stunned. Ynocente's voice had taken on a nonchalant tone and he spoke as if this were another man's plight rather than his own. "They left me less than a man. I could tell no one. Not even you. Until this moment." Ynocente stiffened in the saddle. "Not even my brother knows this sorry secret."

"Consuela's your only daughter—the only child you'll ever have?"

"That is so. You understand why I am so protective of her and why I want only the best for her."

Slocum considered. She would marry her own first cousin if Ynocente had his way. Slocum had heard of stranger marriages, but this struck him as wrong. Maybe this blood wedding wasn't incest in its worst form, but it came damned close.

The hacienda lay ahead. They had returned faster than Slocum had thought possible.

"Do not let this . . . lack of mine affect our friendship. I owe you much, John."

"That doesn't bother me any. I'm sorry for you, Ynocente."

"Do not be sorry," he snapped. "I have a wonderful daughter. She does not know and she must never learn of this. You must swear on your sacred honor."

"I will. But I want you to know—"

Ynocente cut off Slocum's words with a wave of his hand. "Later. We must prepare the fiesta. A celebration! There will be rejoicing. The cattle thieves are dead and Consuela is back where she belongs."

The vaqueros gathered around Ynocente. Slocum teth-ered his stallion and went into the dank, cool interior courtyard of the hacienda. If Ynocente wouldn't listen to him, he would find Consuela and the two of them could slip out during this fiesta. Slocum knew Ynocente would be furious but he could send a telegram from Tucson, or maybe even farther west.

Slocum couldn't let the girl marry her own cousin.

Consuela was not in her room. Slocum went to her *dueña*'s room and found it curiously devoid of life. It took several seconds for him to realize that Consuela's room had been in a similar barren condition. All their personal belongings had been removed and only the heavy mahogany furniture remained.

Slocum searched room after room for Consuela, growing more frantic.

He slammed into Ynocente as he roared into another section of the hacienda.

"John, a word with you."

"Where—"

Again Ynocente Ochoa cut him off. "This is a curious tale I must tell. It is of honor and doing one's duty to family."

Slocum stepped back, his hand resting on the ebony handle of his Colt. Ynocente took no notice. He went to a sideboard, filled two glasses with tequila, and handed one to Slocum. He downed the other one himself, as if giving himself liquid courage, and poured another.

"It is a curious tale of a friend and a lovely woman, a gringo and a *bonita muchacha* and honor and doing what is painful to all but necessary."

"What are you talking about, Ynocente? What have you done?"

Ynocente sipped more slowly at the tequila. "Consuela is a spirited girl and has done much of which I disapprove. I know that she is not a virgin, which makes her less in the eyes of God and my society, but none need know of this." Hot black eyes stared at Slocum.

Slocum looked at the door. Pedro Suarez moved into earshot and stood there, a carbine in his hands. At another door appeared three more vaqueros, all armed.

"She is headstrong and not ready to marry Don Juan's eldest son. For a time, Consuela must learn the virtues of our society."

"Where is she?"

"The convent will give her needed discipline. When she has learned all that is needed from the holy sisters, she will be ready to marry my brother's son."

Slocum rocked slightly, as if a powerful fist had smashed into his belly. Ynocente had sent Consuela away —perhaps to a convent school, as he said, perhaps else-where—and Slocum would never be able to find her. The vaqueros would see to that.

"You were on your way to Tucson when I interrupted your journey. Pedro, give my dear friend the pouch of gold I have prepared. It is small reward for all you have done for me and my *family*," Ynocente said, emphasizing the last word so that Slocum got the message but no one else did. "It is small, but it must suffice. My dear friend, it is for the best. Please believe this."

Slocum took the weighty leather pouch Pedro Suarez handed him. Slocum wanted to blurt out all that Ynocente had told him, how Consuela was really the don's daughter, but he did not.

"Our paths will cross again, Ynocente." Slocum stepped forward. Ynocente tensed. Slocum held out his hand and said, "We will meet again, *amigo*."

Ynocente hugged him, then gently pushed him away. "It is for the best. You may not believe this now, but it is."

Slocum didn't linger on the Ochoa spread. He rode hard, crossing the Rio Grande, and kept riding until exhaustion set in. He camped near Lordsburg, rode hard the next day and the next. By the time Slocum rode across the

Sonora desert and into Tucson, he still hadn't outridden the frustration and anger and loss.

The memory of Consuela faded but the ache remained for a long time.

JAKE LOGAN

J.D. HARDIN

"THE MOST EXCITING
WESTERN WRITER SINCE
LOUIS L'AMOUR"
—JAKE LOGAN

_0-425-07700-4	CARNIVAL OF DEATH #33	$2.50
_0-425-08013-7	THE WYOMING SPECIAL #35	$2.50
_0-425-07257-6	SAN JUAN SHOOTOUT #37	$2.50
_0-425-07259-2	THE PECOS DOLLARS #38	$2.50
_0-425-07114-6	THE VENGEANCE VALLEY #39	$2.75*
_0-425-07386-6	COLORADO SILVER QUEEN #44	$2.50
_0-425-07790-X	THE BUFFALO SOLDIER #45	$2.50
_0-425-07785-3	THE GREAT JEWEL ROBBERY #46	$2.50
_0-425-07789-6	THE COCHISE COUNTY WAR #47	$2.50
_0-425-07974-0	THE COLORADO STING #50	$2.50
_0-425-08088-9	THE CATTLETOWN WAR #52	$2.50
_0-425-08669-0	THE TINCUP RAILROAD WAR #55	$2.50
_0-425-07969-4	CARSON CITY COLT #56	$2.50
_0-425-08743-3	THE LONGEST MANHUNT #59	$2.50
_0-425-08774-3	THE NORTHLAND MARAUDERS #60	$2.50
_0-425-08792-1	BLOOD IN THE BIG HATCHETS #61	$2.50
_0-425-09089-2	THE GENTLEMAN BRAWLER #62	$2.50
_0-425-09112-0	MURDER ON THE RAILS #63	$2.50
_0-425-09300-X	IRON TRAIL TO DEATH #64	$2.50
_0-425-09213-5	THE FORT WORTH CATTLE MYSTERY #65	$2.50
_0-425-09343-3	THE ALAMO TREASURE #66	$2.50
_0-425-09396-4	BREWER'S WAR #67	$2.50
_0-425-09480-4	THE SWINDLER'S TRAIL #68	$2.50
_0-425-09568-1	THE BLACK HILLS SHOWDOWN #69	$2.50
_0-425-09648-3	SAVAGE REVENGE #70	$2.50
_0-425-09713-7	TRAIN RIDE TO HELL #71	$2.50
_0-425-09784-6	THUNDER MOUNTAIN MASSACRE #72	$2.50
_0-425-09895-8	HELL ON THE POWDER RIVER #73	$2.75

Please send the titles I've checked above. Mail orders to:

BERKLEY PUBLISHING GROUP
390 Murray Hill Pkwy., Dept. B
East Rutherford, NJ 07073

NAME_____

ADDRESS_____

CITY_____

STATE_____ZIP_____

Please allow 6 weeks for delivery.
Prices are subject to change without notice.

POSTAGE & HANDLING:
$1.00 for one book, $.25 for each
additional. Do not exceed $3.50.

BOOK TOTAL $_____

SHIPPING & HANDLING $_____

APPLICABLE SALES TAX $_____
(CA, NJ, NY, PA)

TOTAL AMOUNT DUE $_____
PAYABLE IN US FUNDS.
(No cash orders accepted.)